SOMEONE LIKE YOU

ALSO BY MICHELLE DYKMAN

Her Sanctuary, His Heart

The Deal with Dakota

If Only In My Dreams

You, Me, and the Stars
BETHEL PRIVATE SCHOOL SERIES | BOOK ONE

You Found Me
BETHEL PRIVATE SCHOOL SERIES | BOOK THREE

SOMEONE LIKE YOU

MICHELLE DYKMAN

BETHEL PRIVATE SCHOOL SERIES | BOOK TWO

AMBASSADOR INTERNATIONAL
GREENVILLE, SOUTH CAROLINA & BELFAST, NORTHERN IRELAND

www.ambassador-international.com

SOMEONE LIKE YOU

Hardcover ISBN: 978-1-64960-391-3
Paperback ISBN: 978-1-64960-117-9
eISBN: 978-1-64960-167-4
Library of Congress Control Number: 2022936160

Cover design by Hannah Linder Designs
Interior Typesetting by Dentelle Design
Digital Edition by Anna Riebe Raats
Edited by Katie Solomon

AMBASSADOR INTERNATIONAL
Emerald House
411 University Ridge, Suite B14
Greenville, SC 29601, USA
www.ambassador-international.com

AMBASSADOR BOOKS
The Mount
2 Woodstock Link
Belfast, BT6 8DD, Northern Ireland, UK
www.ambassadormedia.co.uk

The colophon is a trademark of Ambassador, a Christian publishing company.

DEDICATION

To all those teen moms who have chosen to give their babies life,
I salute you.

PREFACE

The events in this book run before, parallel, and after the events that take place in *You, Me, and the Stars*. Someone Like You can be read as a standalone; however, I recommend reading the series in order.

For you created my inmost being;
you knit me together in my mother's womb.
I praise you because I am fearfully and wonderfully made;
your works are wonderful,
I know that full well.

Psalm 139:13-14

CHAPTER ONE

Candice Hillman slapped her hand over her mouth, her stomach churning as she flung herself out of bed and stumbled toward the bathroom. The bright flash of the bathroom light blinded her as she rushed to get to the toilet. She barely made it before the contents of her stomach emptied into the bowl.

Her sides ached as she heaved over and over, gasping for breath between each interval and falling to her knees. Eventually, the churning stopped, and exhausted, Candice slid backward and landed with a thump on the cool gray and white tiles. She shivered against the chill on her sweat-soaked body and pulled at her thin sleep shirt.

The floor was cold. Through the bathroom window blinds, she could see the sun peeking out from behind the orange and pink horizon. She took a few deep breaths and rested her head against the cool surface of the white toilet seat. She held her damp hair back with one hand until her heart rate returned to normal. Finally, Candice pushed herself up, standing on shaky feet as she leaned her body against the bathroom cabinet, a white rounded sink set atop a gray, wooden stand, and felt around for a toothbrush.

Brushing quickly and spitting, she called out to her voice-activated alarm clock, "What time is it?"

"The time is now six a.m." A tinny voice replied from the darkness.

Too late to get back into bed if she was going to get the last bit of her history assignment done before today's class. Sighing, she pushed her tired body upright and closed the bathroom door. She turned the shower on, setting it to scalding and wanting desperately to wash away the grimy layer of sweat coating her body. When the water ran cold, she forced herself to dry off and dress for the day.

After rummaging through her extensive wardrobe, Candice decided on dark-wash skinny jeans and a green peasant blouse. She pulled on the clothes and took a few deep breaths as she dressed to calm her roiling stomach. Piling her auburn hair into a messy bun on top of her head, she brushed on a quick layer of makeup. Her stomach still felt too queasy to put much more effort into her appearance. Those enchiladas she'd eaten for supper last night were *not* agreeing with her. Was it the chicken? It did taste funny to her. She'd have to ask Mrs. Potter about it.

She quickly filled her backpack as she bustled around her messy room in search of her textbooks and laptop. After sliding a pile of books into her bag, she turned on her laptop and started on her history homework, losing herself in the marvel of medieval Europe. Once she was done with her assignment, she checked her phone and grimaced. Seven-thirty. She needed to hurry if she was going to eat breakfast before leaving for school. Sliding her feet into her shoes, she zipped her bag closed and hurried down the wooden stairs to the kitchen.

Like every morning, Mrs. Potter was already bustling around with breakfast preparations. Two plates—her mother wasn't back. Again.

"Morning, honey," Mrs. Potter said cheerily.

"Morning. What's for breakfast?" Candice walked around the marble island at the center of the kitchen and sank down into a black bar chair, dropping her bag to the floor beside her.

"You look very pale. Are you feeling all right?" Mrs. Potter asked.

"Yeah, I think so," Candice said, grabbing a cup of coffee from the counter. "I got sick this morning. Do you think it was the chicken? I thought it tasted a bit off."

She took a sip of the drink and grimaced. The coffee tasted a bit weird, too.

Mrs. Potter raised a concerned eyebrow. "The chicken? I hope not, but I'll throw out the leftovers just in case. Would you like some peppermint tea? It works well for an upset stomach."

"Yeah, anything would taste better than this coffee." Candice swallowed hard against a fresh wave of nausea.

Mrs. Potter placed the tea beside her. After a few sips, the warm tea worked its magic, and Candice felt her stomach settle.

"Do you want some breakfast?" Mrs. Potter asked as she rushed around the kitchen.

"Maybe just some toast, please," Candice said. She wasn't sure how much her stomach could handle. "Do you have any idea when my mother will be home?"

"She said sometime this evening."

"Yeah, right," Candice scoffed. If she had a dollar for every time she'd heard that, she would be a millionaire.

"Candice." Mrs. Potter reached over to take Candice's hand. "You know your mother loves you. She's just busy."

"She's always busy. Always too busy for me."

Wasn't that the story of her life? Work always came first for her mother, and everything else always came second, even Candice. No wonder her father had left. The divorce had been amicable—there was no fighting, no ugly court battles. One day, they were a family, and the next day, they weren't. Why her mother wanted custody of her was beyond Candice. She'd rather live with her dad; at least he took an interest in her life. Most days, she wished he lived closer so she could see him more often.

Ever since her parents had divorced four years ago, Candice had been almost completely alone. Her mother had left—perhaps not physically, but definitely emotionally. She still lived in the same house as Candice, but she was rarely ever home. Mrs. Potter, their housekeeper and her unofficial guardian, had become Candice's only company.

Mrs. Potter sighed sympathetically and placed two pieces of buttered toast on the table in front of Candice. "Eat up, honey. It's almost time for school."

Taking small, measured bites in an effort to stop the nausea from returning, Candice ate and drove herself to school.

"Hey, girl, you're early today," her friend Felicia Wren said as she pulled Candice out of her parked car.

"Yeah, rough morning," Candice said. "The house was extra quiet today."

Felicia nodded; she didn't need more explanation than that. Sometimes, Candice wished her parents were more like Felicia's— still together and madly in love. But then again, life didn't always work the way she wanted it to.

"Tell me about it. Alex totally thinks he's in charge while my parents are gone!" Felicia prattled on. Candice knew she loved her brother, but sometimes, their relationship was intense.

She tried to listen to Felicia, but Candice's attention was stolen by a sight that made her heart clench: Brad and Willow. Brad and Willow were laughing outside the main entrance of the school, Willow tossing her long, chestnut hair, and smiling at something Brad said with flirtatious enthusiasm.

"Candice, are you listening?" Felicia asked, snapping her fingers in front of Candice's face.

Candice jumped and turned back to Felicia. "What? I mean, yeah," she lied.

"Oh, yeah? What did I just say?" Felicia crossed her arms over her chest, a slight frown marring her brow. The wind ruffled her wild, brown hair, and fire shot from her blue eyes. Then, she saw what Candice had been focused on, and her smile turned down at the corners. "He loves you," she said, tapping Candice on the shoulder. It was a sympathetic gesture. They both knew what Willow was capable of.

Before, Candice might have believed it, but Brad had been so strange the last few times they'd been together. She wasn't so sure anymore. But as if to erase her fears, Brad's eyes met hers, and his face lit up. He excused himself from Willow and hurried over to her, smiling broadly.

"Hey, babe," he said, pressing his soft lips against hers.

Candice's doubt disappeared, and she wrapped her arm around his waist, breathing in his fresh, clean scent.

"Hey, you." She returned his kiss with enthusiasm, ignoring the disgruntled expression marring Willow's beautiful face as she pulled away.

Go find your own, Willow.

Wild Willow could have any guy she wanted. She had better keep her hands off Candice's.

"I'll see you later," Felicia said with a suggestive wink, and Candice felt her face heat.

Brad chuckled and bent his head to hers again, snagging another quick kiss. Brad broke the kiss and led them into the busy school building. The hallway bustled with various members of the student body at Bethel Private School. The pale white walls lined with dull, gray lockers rang with the sound of laughter, arguing, and slamming doors. The air smelled the same as it did every day—like old sweat and cleaning detergent.

"Did you have a good night?" Brad asked, looping his arm around her waist and shielding her from oncoming students.

"It would have been better if you'd spent it with me," Candice said. Then, she snuck in the words she really wanted to say. "So, did Willow need something from you?"

"Sorry, babe, I wanted to come over, but practice comes first. Plus, my dad wanted me to—Wait, Willow?" Brad cast confused eyes over to Candice.

"Earlier, when you were at the door with her, did she want something?" Candice clarified, trying to sound casual.

"What? No. She was asking about Connor and the practice schedule."

"Oh, okay." Candice shrugged, not fully appeased. "Anyway, what were you saying your dad wanted?"

Brad's expression turned sour. "Oh, you know. Same old, same old. Never satisfied with anything I do or don't do."

Brad pulled her closer into his side. She was his comfort. There'd been many times where she'd held him after an argument with his dad, Adrian Thorn.

"Just for once, I wish you would stand up to your dad," she said.

Preaching to the choir, Candice.

Brad sighed, his smile slipping. It was an old argument between Brad and his dad—Brad trying to be independent, his dad insisting on perfection. He shook his head. "It doesn't ever help," he shrugged "I don't waste my time anymore."

"Never mind. You're here now, and that's all that matters." She laid a swift kiss on him and hoped the teachers patrolling the hallways wouldn't catch them. Nobody needed a trip to Principal Rory on a Monday morning.

Brad paused, his expression intense. Something shadowed his deep blue eyes. But as quickly as it came, the expression disappeared. He smiled again and kissed her cheek.

"Yeah. We'd better hurry. I don't think Aria would be too pleased if we're late for class again."

Candice followed Brad, cheeks flushed and quietly giggling about the time Mrs. Aria had caught them kissing behind the gym door. Maybe she didn't need to worry about Willow after all.

CHAPTER TWO

At the door they separated, Candice to her human development class and Brad to his science class. It was strange to remember how they had barely known each other at the beginning of the year. But strangers had quickly become friends, and over time, that friendship had grown into what Candice considered love.

Mrs. Aria, the human development teacher, called the class to attention with a loud whistle.

"To continue on from our last class, when does a fertilized egg become a baby?" Mrs. Aria asked the class.

"When there's a heartbeat?" Cindy guessed in her timid voice.

"At conception." That was Paulette. She was one of the smart ones always ahead of the rest of the class.

"At twelve weeks?" Amy said from the back.

The class fell silent, and Mrs. Aria looked around expectantly.

"Anyone else?" she asked.

Still more silence.

"Okay, when will a woman consider herself pregnant?" she asked.

"When she takes a test?" another girl asked.

"When she's missed a period," Paulette said.

There were some spatters of giggles, and "Gross!" echoed from a couple of the boys.

Candice shook her head, faintly bemused by their behavior. The boys had a lot of growing up to do.

Some of them, anyway, she thought.

"Okay. As this is a Christian school, we will look at what the Bible has to say about when a life is a life." Mrs. Aria pointed to a dark blue book that lay on her desk.

A cacophony of voices filled the class, each student shouting out their opinion.

"All right, settle down. Turn to Psalm 100, verse three in your Bibles." She paused for a moment, allowing the students to turn to the relevant verses.

"'Know that the LORD is God. It is he who made us, and we are his; we are his people, the sheep of his pasture.'" She held her place with one hand. "What does this tell us about our lives?"

Paulette shifted in her seat. Candice rolled her eyes. The girl seemed to know everything.

"Yes, Paulette?" Mrs. Aria asked

"The verse shows that God made us," Paulette said.

Paulette said the words so confidently that Candice couldn't help but sigh. Paulette was a loud-and-proud Christian, and while Candice didn't necessarily have a problem with it, she still wasn't so sure about the whole "Christian" thing. The only reason she was at a Christian school like Bethel was because her mom had forced her to come when they'd moved here last year.

"Thank you, Paulette," Mrs. Aria said. "Now, let's turn to Isaiah 44, verse twenty-four: 'This is what the Lord says—your Redeemer, who formed you in the womb: I am the Lord, the Maker of all things, who stretches out the heavens, who spreads out the earth by myself.' So, this verse tells us again that God made us, but what else does it tell us?" Mrs. Aria asked.

Hands flew up. Paulette again. "That He formed us in the womb?"

"Yes, and what does this tell us about when a fertilized egg becomes a baby?"

Silence rang like a bell through the room.

Mrs. Aria touched the book on her desk. "It tells us that life begins the moment of conception. A baby is formed in that moment, not a random clump of cells or potential life. A living, breathing, growing human being."

For the rest of the lesson, Mrs. Aria read verses from the Bible and explained what she thought they meant, but Candice was more preoccupied with Willow and Brad's interaction that morning. Was it really as simple as Brad said it was? She never could be sure after all the stories she'd heard around school about Willow's previous exploits. Willow had a track record that would make any girl wonder whether she was after her boyfriend. She was known for boyfriend-stealing, among other things.

Candice blew out a noisy breath, and she tried to concentrate on what Mrs. Aria was saying; but by this time, she'd moved onto DNA and family ancestry, and Candice was hopelessly lost. As soon as the bell rang, Candice quickly packed up her bags, itching to escape the classroom.

"Hey, babe," Brad said, sauntering over to her with a smile. "Can I walk you to Dempster?" His hand settled at the small of her spine, and she reveled in the contact.

"Yeah, I guess." Her brain felt fuzzy, and she blinked a few times to clear her vision. Mr. Dempster's history class was on the other side of the school. "You know what? Don't worry about it. I don't want to make you late for shop class again; Coach wouldn't like it."

Brad grimaced. "Yeah, I guess. I could still make it if I ran."

"Brad, its fine." She didn't want Brad to get into trouble with his dad again. If there was another phone call home, who knew what would happen to him.

"You sure?"

"Yeah, go. I'll see you at lunch."

"Okay. Miss you." Brad kissed her quickly and rushed off to his next class.

Candice hurried toward Mr. Dempster's class when the smell of food cooking wafted through the hall from the Home Economics class. Her stomach lurched again, nausea rising in her throat. Gasping, she raced for the bathroom and dry-heaved in the nearest cubicle.

"Are you okay?" Amy Carter, another one of Candice's friends, came out of the stall beside hers.

"Yeah, I'm fine. I ate something bad last night, and now I'm paying for it." She cupped her hand under the tap and took a few swallows, swishing the water in her mouth before spitting it out.

"Man, that's too bad. Do you need me to call your mom?"

"Nah, I'll just go to the office and ask if I can go home. I'm still not feeling great. Would you tell Brad at lunch when you see him?"

"Sure, no problem. Let me walk you to the office."

Amy walked Candice to the school office, leaving her there with a wave and a pitying smile.

"Candice, do you need something?" Mrs. Fredericks, the school receptionist, looked up from her computer and watched from behind her glasses balanced on the edge of her nose.

"Yeah, I need to go home. I think I have food poisoning."

"Oh, dear! Sure, let's get you signed out."

Mrs. Fredericks pulled a file from the cabinet and flipped through the roster. Candice signed her name.

"I hope you feel better soon," she said kindly.

"Thank you," Candice said over her shoulder as she hurried out to her car.

The drive home was swift, and the buzz of the vacuum cleaner greeted Candice when pushed open the front door.

"Mrs. Potter?" she called, closing the door behind her.

The vacuum cleaner shut off, and Mrs. Potter came bustling around the corner into the hallway.

"Candice? What are you doing home?" she asked.

"I feel gross, and my stomach doesn't want to settle," Candice said wearily. "I think I need to lie down."

"You go ahead; I'll bring you some more tea."

With a muttered thanks, Candice dragged her tired body up to her room and was out the moment her head hit the pillow.

The sunlight had moved across the sky by the time Candice opened her eyes. Morning was long past, and the afternoon was well on its way to evening.

Groaning softly, she pushed her mess of hair back from her sweaty face; her throat was parched, and her stomach grumbled with hunger. A cooled cup of tea rested on her bedside table. She sipped it before making a trip to the bathroom. Yawning, Candice padded down the stairs. The smooth finish of the wooden handrail used to calm her, but today, it reminded her of the emptiness in her life. Shiny and lifeless.

"Candice?" Mrs. Potter called from somewhere in the house. The lavishly decorated living room awaited Candice at the bottom of the staircase. Wide bay windows delicately draped in white and soft gray curtains. A modern, white sofa set spread across the room like one side of a giant rectangle. On the floor lay a darker gray rug. Everything of the best quality for her mother.

"Coming," Candice answered.

Mrs. Potter appeared in the southern archway of the room. Her dark, Mediterranean hair was pulled into an elaborate braid running around the top of her head and off behind her right shoulder. As usual, she was dressed in her comfortable, beige capri pants and colorful t-shirt, and Candice was suddenly grateful for the comforting stability that was Mrs. Potter.

"Goodness, Candice, have you been sleeping this entire time?" Soft, brown eyes gazed inquiringly at her.

"Yeah. I don't know why I'm so exhausted." Raising her hands above her head, she stretched out the kinks in her neck and let out another long yawn.

"Are you hungry?"

"Starving!" Candice rested her elbows on the black marble countertop, holding her head in her hands. Another long yawn escaped her.

A side plate with a ham and cheese sandwich slid under her arms. Candice sat back into her chair and ate, sipping the fresh cup of tea Mrs. Potter placed beside the plate.

"Thank you for looking after me," Candice said.

"Anytime, dear. Are you still feeling sick?" Mrs. Potter busied herself with making her own tea before taking a seat.

"No, I feel fine now. I think I might go and enjoy the sunlight a bit."

"That sounds like an excellent idea. Remember to take water with you."

"Yes, 'Mom,'" Candice said teasingly, although the words were truer than anything.

Trainers on and water bottle in a small pouch on her hip, Candice walked out into the late afternoon light. A slight, balmy breeze blew, bringing with it the scent of jasmine flowers. Walking at a steady pace, she made her way down the long driveway and out onto the sidewalk, heading toward the park a few blocks down.

Candice had only just entered the green expanse of grass when a sudden cramp rippled across her stomach, causing her to double over. Stumbling over to the nearest park bench, she sat down and breathed slowly through the pain. Maybe she wasn't as over the food poisoning as she thought.

Her head swam, and curtains of blackness crept along the outer edges of her vision, pulling slowly shut. Blinking rapidly, she tried to stop their movement only to fall deeper into their persistent blackness.

CHAPTER THREE

"**M**iss? Hey, Miss, are you okay?"

A male voice pulled Candice out of her faint. It had a nice warmth to it, like drinking warm cocoa.

"Hey, Miss, can you open your eyes? Are you okay?"

Blinking slowly, Candice opened her eyes to see a boy with a concerned face hovering over her. She found herself distracted by the depth and kindness of his blue eyes before the reality of the situation struck her. Why was the boy's face above hers? And why did she feel grass beneath her when she was sure she had been sitting on a bench?

You fainted, remember?

"Hey," the boy said. "Are you okay?"

He wrapped a strong hand under one of her elbows and placed the other in her hand, helping her to her feet.

"Yeah, I . . . uh . . . I think so." Her head spun, and she stumbled again. The boy braced her forearms with both his hands; her skin tingled beneath his touch.

"Perhaps not," he said. "Maybe you should sit down."

He gently tugged her down onto the wooden bench. Darkness crept over her eyes again, and she blinked rapidly. This time, the darkness was swept back. The boy let go of her and sat back onto the bench, retrieving something from beside him.

"Here, drink up." The boy handed her a bottle of water, and she gratefully took a few mouthfuls. He watched her, concern etched between his brows.

"Hey, don't I know you from somewhere?" he asked. His eyes sparked with excitement, and Candice found herself distracted again by the blueness in them.

Stop it, Candice. Pretty eyes aside, did he really just use a pickup line on me after I fainted?

Candice grimaced, and the boy frowned.

"No, seriously, that wasn't some cheesy pickup line!" he said. "I'm sure I've seen you before."

Now he could read minds, too?

The boy's expression brightened as if a lightbulb had just gone off. "Mr. Phillips, third period, right? Math?"

Of course. What were the odds she'd be rescued by someone who went to Bethel?

"What's your name again?" he asked.

Candice gave him a small smile. "Candice Hillman."

"Jack Anson," he said, extending his hand again to shake hers. His dirty blond hair tangled in the breeze, and his expression was kind and happy.

"It's nice to meet you, Jack."

"It's nice to meet you, too, Candice," he said cheerily. Then, his expression sobered. "How's the head feeling? You took a nasty tumble back there."

"It's all right," she said, pressing her fingertips gingerly against her head and testing it for tenderness. "A bit sore but okay. Thanks."

They sat for a moment, enjoying the peacefulness of the park. Jack bounced a basketball between his legs as if he had nowhere else in the world to be.

Candice felt his gaze on her, and embarrassment began to creep in. "I feel much better now," she said, feeling flushed. "Thank you for helping me, Jack."

Candice jumped up from the bench to leave, but as soon as she stood, she felt her blood rush to her feet and her vision dim and she felt herself stumbling. Jack leaped to his feet and took hold of her arm in a firm grasp to steady her.

"Hey, hang on there," he cautioned, guiding her back onto the bench.

"I'm fine, really." Candice braced her elbows on her knees and squeezed the bridge of her nose between two fingers. Truthfully, she felt awful.

"Can I give you a ride home?" he asked.

"No, you don't need to worry. I don't live far from here, and I like walking." Candice's embarrassment heightened.

"It's no hassle; let me walk you home! Besides, you don't look very steady on your feet. Are you sure you don't want to sit down a bit longer?" Again, tingles swept down her arms from the spot where his hand rested on her shoulder.

"No, I think I need to go home," she said. Determined to ignore the strange sensations this boy arose in her, she stepped out from under his hand.

Jack sighed. "Look, think of it this way. You can take my giant-size hero complex and let me walk you home, or I can just follow behind you. What will it be?" He held his hands out in appeal to her, his jaw set. This was an argument she wasn't winning.

"Fine." Candice turned on her heel, ready to march home. Her breath caught slightly when Jack's warm hand cupped her elbow and led her to the sidewalk.

"Was that so hard?"

"Excruciating," she joked dryly as Jack fell in step beside. He released her elbow but stayed close. He bounced the basketball as they walked.

"So, how long have you lived in Bethel?" The *thump, thump, thump* of the basketball punctuated his question.

"Just over four years now. We moved here when my parents split."

"Man, I'm sure that was hard."

"I miss my dad. As for my mom, well, she's never around anymore."

Jack hummed sympathetically. "I'm sorry to hear that. Do you still see your dad?"

"Every two weeks. He lives in another town. I see him on weekends, but we talk almost every day." Searching for a change of topic, Candice nodded her head toward the basketball in Jack's hand. "Do you play?"

"Yeah. League and at the community center. That's actually where I was when I saw you pass out."

"Oh no," she groaned. "I'm sure it was spectacular." She laughed and smoothed an errant hair, imagining in vivid color her graceless collapse and how ridiculous she must've looked.

"Definitely Oscar-worthy."

She liked this boy. He was easy to talk to, and she thought that she might be able to make a new friend.

Jack walked with Candice back to her house, stopping to gape at the massive structure as they came to a stop. "You live here?" Disbelief and awe laced his question.

"Yeah, I know. It's huge." She shrugged. She was used to the vastness of her house. It did little to impress her anymore.

She studied the house disinterestedly. It was a colonial double-story, with large bay windows and an impressive hardwood door. The gardens teemed with color, sloping toward a wrap around patio. It was beautiful, even if the beauty was only on the outside. She'd give anything to go back to the small, two-bedroom bungalow in Westwood if it meant having a family again.

"You okay?" he asked. His blue eyes, so deep and vivid, studied her face. It was as if he really saw her. Saw *through* her.

"Yeah. Thanks for walking me home," she said, dodging his concern. Candice felt oddly at ease with him—unexplainably so—but still, she wasn't ready to tell him about all of her baggage.

They walked down the long driveway only to be met by a furious sight. Brad was slouched against the hood of his car, his face red and his body rigid with anger. A nervous flutter entered her stomach. What was Brad doing here?

"So, I come to check on you, and this is what I find? You and Jack Anson? Are you even sick?" Brad yelled.

"Brad, wait. This isn't—" Candice's voice wavered. What was happening here?

Jack stepped between them "It's nothing, I found her in the park. She passed out."

Brad's hands unclenched, the ruddy color in his cheeks paling. "You passed out? I'm sorry, babe. Are you okay?"

Remorse covered his handsome face, and Candice instantly forgave his rash assumptions. After all, hadn't she reacted the same way when she saw Willow and Brad talking that morning at school? Brad's arms encircled her, and she sank into his embrace. The usual comfort she found in his arms was missing.

"I'm all right. Jack offered to walk me home after I woke up," she said.

"Sorry, man. Thanks for looking out for her," Brad said, pulling away from Candice to extend a hand to Jack.

"No problem." Jack shook Brad's hand, unease marring his forehead. His eyes flickered to Candice. "I'll see you tomorrow in math, Candice?"

Candice nodded, ignoring the way Brad tightened his hold on her.

"Candice. Brad." Jack nodded one last time and walked back up the drive, disappearing around the boundary wall.

"Are you sure you're okay?" Brad placed a soft kiss on her forehead.

"Yeah, I think I have the stomach flu or something. I'll be okay."

"Okay, well, if you're okay, then I have to go. I have practice, and there's no way my dad would let me skip."

Candice blinked. "But you just got here."

"I know. I'm sorry."

With a quick kiss, Brad climbed into his car and sped away, leaving Candice standing alone in the driveway with her emotions in a confused knot and her thoughts in a blur.

Jack's smile slipped away as he walked down the street to the community center. Poor Candice. He hoped she felt better soon, and he hoped that Brad didn't make things worse. Jack had no idea what she—or any other girls—saw in Brad, anyway. The way Brad had yelled at Candice made Jack's blood boil. She didn't deserve that, and she also didn't deserve a boyfriend who was unfaithful to her—that is, of course, if the rumors about Brad and Willow were true.

Coach stood beside the court, a bemused expression on his angular face. Coach Nick wasn't a huge man; he was short and lean for a basketball player, but he knew the game like he knew his own name.

"Where have you been, Anson?" he asked, tossing Jack the nearest basketball.

"Just helping out a damsel in distress," he joked. Inside, though, he was sighing, caught up in thoughts of wild, auburn hair; clear, brown eyes; and a smile that made his heart beat like a jack hammer.

"Yeah, yeah. One day that knight in shining armor complex is going to get you into trouble."

"It hasn't yet!" Jack smirked, forcing a laugh from Coach.

"Give it time, Prince Charming."

Jack laughed. "Ready when you are, Coach!"

Coach blew his whistle, drawing the other guys' attention. "Huddle in, team. Let's get to work . . . "

CHAPTER FOUR

The next morning was a dreadful repeat of the previous one. After a short breakfast and two cups of peppermint tea to quell her nausea, Candice was off to school. If this didn't stop soon, she would need to see a doctor. This couldn't be normal.

"Hey, Candice! Are you okay? I heard you went home early yesterday." Felicia's shadow passed over the hood of Candice's car. Candice thrust the door open and climbed out.

"Yeah, I'm fine, thanks. Just a bit of stomach flu. I'm feeling much better now, though." Well, she did feel better—sort of.

She looked around for Brad. Once again, he stood by the entrance of the school, laughing with Willow. Her hand was wrapped around his strong bicep, and her head lay comfortably on his shoulder. Closing the door with more force than necessary, Candice stormed over to the school.

"What are you doing?" Candice said. Willow swung around, the smile on her face slowly fading. Brad's eyes went wide, and he quickly shook Willow away and took a large step toward Candice.

"Babe, nothing's going on." Brad took her hand in his and pulled her closer. Confusion spiraled inside her. Maybe she was overreacting, but she thought Brad sounded guiltier than he should.

Willow rolled her eyes. "Whatever, I'm out of here." She flipped her long hair, turned on her heel, and sauntered into the school.

"I'll see you inside," Felicia said, graciously giving Candice and Brad some space. Candice had only known Felicia a short time, yet the sympathetic look she threw over her shoulder as she walked away spoke volumes.

"Brad. What is this?" Candice gestured wildly with her hands. Tears blurred her vision and made Brad's shame-filled face swim before her eyes.

"Nothing, babe. I swear! You know Willow—she's always so handsy," he said.

Sadly, that was true. Willow felt the need to mark her property everywhere she went, kind of like a lioness prowling around her territory. Candice felt sick; this time it wasn't the unrelenting swirling in her stomach but a deep sinking in her heart. Was she losing Brad to Willow?

"I'm sorry," she whispered. This was too much for her to handle, and she didn't want to put any other stress on Brad, especially when he already felt so distant from her lately. "Let's just forget it happened, okay?"

Brad smiled, looking relieved. Candice's stomach twisted into knots.

"Of course. Come on, babe, you know you're the only one for me." He kissed her softly and led her down the busy corridor and into Mrs. Aria's class right as the first bell rang.

"Continuing on from our discussion about genes and hormones," Mrs. Aria said, "today, we will look at how a woman's body changes to accommodate a growing baby and some of the accompanying symptoms. For example, one of the symptoms many women will experience during the first few months of pregnancy is morning sickness. Although there are no official known causes of morning sickness, doctors speculate that an increase in hormones is to blame."

Mrs. Aria's voice faded into the background as her words slowly penetrated Candice's mind. Could it be? Was she? No, she couldn't be. It was only the one time.

All it takes is one time, a voice whispered to her.

Where had she heard that before? She couldn't remember. But, still, she couldn't be . . . She couldn't even think of the word.

How do you explain the sickness in the morning and yesterday afternoon? The voice said again.

She'd had food poisoning from the chicken she'd had for dinner. That was all. She couldn't be pregnant. But as Mrs. Aria droned on in the background, Candice could feel the pit in her stomach get heavier by the second.

"Babe, are you okay?" Brad asked sometime during lunch, shaking Candice from her stupor. Judging by the edge in his voice, he'd been asking for a while.

"Uh, sorry, what?" The lunchroom was fuller than when they'd sat down. Their friends sat around them, eating and joking.

"Candice, where is your head today? You've barely said two words all lunch," he said.

"I'm sorry. I have a lot on my mind."

A shadow passed over Brad's face again. It looked remarkably like the expression he'd had when she saw him with Willow that morning.

"Anything I can do?" He slid his arm carefully around her shoulders, just stealthily enough that hopefully the teachers wandering in and out of the lunchroom wouldn't notice.

"No, I think I'm okay. I haven't really been sleeping well. Anyway, how was football practice?"

"Great! Coach showed us this really cool play . . . " And he went off on a tangent. Candice sighed in relief; one thing Brad loved to talk about was football.

The lunch bell rang, and Candice treaded tiredly to her next class. Brad had to run to his class across campus, so she was alone. She heard voices whispering furiously and slowed down, creeping to the corner of the hallway. She turned her head around the corner and saw Felicia and Willow, heads bent close.

"I wish he would just leave her. I know he wants to be with me." There was no mistaking the venom in Willow's voice. Candice put her hand to her mouth to stifle her gasp.

"Will, leave the guy alone. You know he loves her. He might mess around with you every now and then, but at the end of the day, he's going to stay with her."

Willow huffed. "Not if I have anything to say about it."

Candice whipped back around the corner and hurried to Mr. Phillips' classroom, Willow and Felicia's conversation whirling through her head. Willow was talking about Brad. She had to be! Candice wouldn't put it past Willow to chase after someone who was already in a relationship, but surely, Brad wouldn't accept her advances. At least, Candice didn't think he would. He loved Candice . . . Right?

Memories from the last two mornings suddenly looked different to her. The closeness between Willow and Brad. Was there more to it? Lost in thought, Candice didn't see the tall figure in front of her until she bumped her nose into its chest.

"Sorry," she mumbled, head bent low as her thoughts swirled in chaos.

"Hey, Candice," a familiar voice greeted her. Candice jerked her head up to see Jack's amused face.

"Oh! Hey, Jack," she said in surprise.

"Looks like there are some serious thoughts bouncing around in that pretty head of yours. Is something bothering you?" Jack stepped back, putting some space between them to look at her properly.

Candice sighed and forced a smile. "No, I'm doing okay," she assured, trying to ignore the heaviness in her heart at the same time. "How are you today?"

Jack grinned. "Doing okay. You?"

Candice curled her arms around her middle. Was she okay? She didn't know. Forcing a bright smile, she nodded. "Yeah. Good."

"Are you sure?" He waited for her to confirm or deny his statement. When she didn't answer, he sighed. "So, I wanted to ask you something. There's a fundraiser basketball game on Thursday at the community center, and I was wondering if you'd like to come. All sales go to Walker Clinic for Children."

"That sounds like a great cause," Candice said, her spirits lifting in response to Jack's smile. "Are you playing?"

"Yeah! Do you want to bring anyone? My mom and dad will be there, too."

Candice's thoughts drifted back to Brad—she could bring him. As his girlfriend, she probably *should* bring him. But after today, Candice wasn't sure her heart could handle seeing him so soon.

"No," Candice decided. "I'll come by myself. It's sounds like a fun time," she said with a smile.

"Awesome! Do you want to meet me at the basketball court in the middle of town?" Jack sheepishly rubbed the back of his neck. "I would offer to pick you up, but then it might sound too much like a date."

Candice laughed lightly, rolling her eyes at Jack. "Sounds like a plan," she said, grateful for this boy who was able to bring sunshine to others so easily.

"Class, come to order," Mr. Phillips called from the front of the room. Mr. Phillips was a tall, thin man with black hair that stuck out wildly in all directions. As disorganized as his hair was, he was a great teacher. Sadly, math was still Candice's worst subject. As the lesson wore on, she found herself more and more confused by the theorems and equations Mr. Phillips wrote on the board.

"Hey." Jack turned in his seat and gestured to her blank assignment sheet. "How are you doing with this lesson?" He'd moved from his seat across the room to the one beside her.

Candice shrugged. "Needless to say, I have no idea what I'm supposed to be doing."

"I can help if you want," Jack said kindly.

"Thank you, but it's all right. I'm sure you have enough on your plate." She studied the squiggles and lines on the board. They looked like an elaborate abstract painting to Candice, but she vainly hoped that if she stared at them long enough, they'd magically make sense.

"Okay. Let me know if you change your mind." Jack smiled and turned back to the front of the class, his hand moving rapidly across the assignment sheet. Candice sighed; she wished she could be as good at math as she was at art or history.

When the final bell rang, a wave of nausea centered Candice's thoughts on her human development class.

Accepting that she couldn't deny the unease in her stomach any longer, Candice drove to the nearby drug store. Her heart rate quickened as she pulled to a stop and climbed out of her car. She tried to hold her head high and put on an air of confidence, but the shaking in her legs and the sweat on her palms betrayed her nervousness.

Candice took a deep breath and pushed open the drug store door. The cheerful ding of the doorbell sounded like the signal for her doom.

She walked down the long, white aisles filled with products. The sign for the planned parenthood section glared at her, and she circled the aisle, stalling desperately in an attempt to build up courage. Eventually, she braved the aisle. She walked up, turned, and walked down, and then turned around again, finally coming to a stop in front of the pregnancy tests. And turned to leave again.

Stop being silly, Candice, just do it. The test will come back negative, and life will go on.

That was the hope, wasn't it?

But what if it's positive?

Her pulse rocketed. Ignoring the voices in her head pushing her in two different directions, Candice grabbed the nearest package and marched to the cashier. Aside from a raised eyebrow, the cashier said nothing. She handed Candice her package and whispered, "Good luck, honey."

Candice kept her eyes low, the package burning in her hand as she left the store and tossed it in the passenger seat of her car. As she drove home, Candice gripped the steering wheel tightly and tried to ignore the foreboding feeling in her stomach that her entire life was about to change.

CHAPTER FIVE

For the next few days, Candice denied the feeling in her gut that told her what the result would be if she took that test. It was like the constant chiming of a clock, in the mornings as she hung over the toilet, until she could deny it no longer.

Unceremoniously, she grabbed the pregnancy test she'd been hiding for the last few days and walked into the bathroom. The test shook in her hands as she pulled out the plastic stick, letting the box drop to the ground beside her. Her stomach twisted and squirmed. The harmless looking stick trembled as she took the test and laid it on the basin beside her. She washed up and set her phone to five minutes. On unsteady legs, she hobbled back into her bedroom, pacing from her window to her door, once, twice, thrice and checking her phone at each pass. The knot pulled tighter and tighter as the minutes passed. Waves of nausea clawed up her throat. Candice breathed deeply and tried to shake the tingles from her fingers—the timer on her phone went off, and she froze.

Her five minutes were up. The moment of truth had come.

She took a deep breath and walked back into the bathroom. The small, white stick waited innocently for her on the basin. Innocent, yet with the ability to change her life in a moment's notice.

Candice picked up the test and looked at the results.

Two bright, pink lines glared back at her.

The test tumbled to the floor. Candice watched it fall, taking with it all her hopes and dreams. She'd never spoken to anyone about those dreams for the future. Her secret desire to learn about the human mind, to somehow understand why her parents were no longer married. Why she lived in two families instead of one. Why her mother didn't love her anymore. Now she would never find those answers. Now those dreams were dust.

She fell to her knees, losing the contents of her stomach over the lip of the toilet.

After a few minutes, Candice pushed herself away from the toilet and wiped her mouth; her stomach had stopped roiling, but now, it was her mind that spun. Candice wasn't dumb enough to believe that there wouldn't be a consequence of her choice, but it had only been the one time. The one time she'd said yes and had sex with Brad.

What were the odds that she would have to pay such a high price for her stupidity?

Tears slid down her cheeks; she tried to wipe them away, but the torrent quickly overpowered her shaking hands. Her head swirled. The shaking moved from her hands into her arms, racing up until her whole body shook. She gritted her teeth, not making a sound, although everything inside her wanted to wail and whimper in defeat.

What have I done?

The door to the bathroom opened, and the bright light from the hallway pressed into the miserable depths.

"Candice, are you all right?" Mrs. Potter gently pressed the door open further. Seeing Candice huddled on the tile floor, Mrs. Potter walked over and perched herself on the rim of the nearby bathtub.

Her black hair gleamed softly in the fluorescent light, and the familiar smell of lemon and sunshine filled Candice's nose.

"What is it, Candice?" She laid her soft hands, always filled with love, on Candice's bowed head.

"I'm pregnant." Her words floated through the air, but their implications settled like a heavy weight on her shoulders.

A baby. She was going to have a baby. Horror filled her, and disbelief followed. But the small, white test with the bold, pink lines didn't lie.

Mrs. Potter didn't gasp; she didn't even stiffen. She merely bent down and wrapped Candice into a tight embrace. Candice pressed her face deep into Mrs. Potter's shoulder and wept.

"Oh, my little Candice. Don't worry. It will be all right," she soothed, gently running her hands through Candice's tangled auburn hair.

For a moment, Candice believed her. For a moment, she could almost feel that it would be all right, but then she'd look at the test again, and the reality of her choice would tell her a different answer. What would she tell her father? And her mother? Would her mother even care?

"Come on, let's get you up." Mrs. Potter helped Candice to her feet. The room spun, and Candice clamped her hands onto Mrs. Potter's forearms.

"I'm a bit dizzy," Candice muttered. Blackness seeped into her eyes. Candice struggled to blink it away. Her head felt light.

Mrs. Potter's brow puckered. "I think you need a lie down. When was the last time you ate?"

"I think at school," Candice guessed. "I wasn't feeling too well last night."

"Is that why you bought one of those?" Mrs. Potter glanced down at the positive pregnancy test on the ground.

"Yeah," Candice sighed.

"Well, there's no use crying over spilled milk now, my dear. We just need to move forward," Mrs. Potter soothed.

Candice felt a wave of relief wash over her at the word "we"—it felt so good for someone to be by her side. Candice was so used to being alone. Ever since her dad had left and her mom had begun traveling across the globe, Candice had been given the job of raising herself with only Mrs. Potter to keep her company. And as much as she loved and appreciated Mrs. Potter, she couldn't help but feel isolated and abandoned by the people she should have been able to depend upon the most.

That being said, Candice was very glad that, at least for today, her mother wasn't here to witness this.

"What am I going to do?" she asked miserably.

Mrs. Potter sighed. "Right now, we're going to go down to the kitchen and get you some tea and crackers. After that, we can decide what to do."

Candice held fast to Mrs. Potter as she led her out of the bathroom and to the kitchen, feeling steadier in Mrs. Potter's arms. Mrs. Potter pulled out one of the bar chairs beside the marble kitchen island.

"Sit." She pointed to the chair and walked over to the kettle. She waited in silence as Mrs. Potter brewed the tea and placed a steaming cup in front of Candice.

"Is it that boy?" Mrs. Potter asked.

Candice swallowed. "It's Brad."

Frowning, Mrs. Potter took a sip of her tea, grimaced, and then added a spoonful of sugar and a dash of milk. Mrs. Potter liked her tea like the English: sweet and milky. A small smile bloomed on Candice's mouth. The sight of Mrs. Potter's tea was familiar and comforting, even when the world felt like it was collapsing underneath her.

"I see," she said and took another sip. "Does he know?"

Candice shook her head; she'd been afraid to speculate with Brad about her morning sickness. Afraid of how he'd react, especially since their relationship was on shaky ground already. Brad wanted more than she was willing to give, and she couldn't really blame him for growing impatient with her. She'd never denied him much until that night when one kiss had led to more, and more kisses had led to . . . this.

"How far along do you think you are?" Mrs. Potter took a sip of her tea and set it down on the saucer.

"I'm not sure . . . About eight weeks, I think?" Candice didn't need to guess. She knew without a doubt it was eight weeks. She'd only ever had sex once, and she could remember the exact time, date, and any other detail of that night. That night where one lapse in judgment lead to her to becoming a teenage statistic.

"You should tell him . . . " Mrs. Potter paused. "It would be useless for me to say I told you so, but Candice . . . "

"I know, I know. I should have listened to you. Still, he's nice and charming, and he makes me feel . . . " Her voice trailed off. Brad made her feel warm, loved, and special. Although . . . Lately, she was feeling a bit more neglected by Brad than she would like to admit. Truthfully, right now, the thought of Brad made her feel anxious. Anxious that he would leave her for Willow. Anxious that he was falling out of love with her. Anxious that he would reject her when he found out he was going to be a dad.

Dad.

The word revolted in Candice's stomach, her heart beating heavily inside her chest, pounding a rhythm through her blood. Her hands became clammy, and she wiped them on her pajama pants and sucked in deep breaths. Her dad would be so disappointed.

"Candice?" Mrs. Potter jumped to her feet and raced around the table. Her firm hand landed on Candice's shoulder. "Deep breaths. It's okay. It's okay," she soothed, her voice calm.

Candice forced herself to listen to Mrs. Potter's words and time her breaths with them. In. Out. It's okay. It's okay. After some time, her racing heart calmed, and her breathing returned to normal.

"There you go. Calm. You are okay." Her hand rubbed soothing circles into Candice's back. "Just breathe."

Candice picked up her tea, the hot liquid shaking in unison with her hand, and took a small sip. She didn't have words right now for how epically freaked out she was. She was going to have a baby. What did she know about being a mom?

Maybe . . . maybe she could make it go away? Get rid of it before anyone else found out.

No. She recoiled at the thought. She couldn't do that.

But she couldn't possibly *have* the baby either! Oh, she didn't know what to do. Should she even tell Brad? Would he break up with her? It had been Brad's first time, too—surely that meant something. She wouldn't lose him to this. Would she?

Mrs. Potter's dark eyes watched as Candice's brain whirled, patiently waiting while Candice thought. Finally, she looked at Mrs. Potter.

"I think . . . " she began. "I think I need to make an appointment to see a doctor."

Mrs. Potter smiled. "I think that's a good idea. I know a wonderful OB/GYN."

Candice shook her head, watching the expression on Mrs. Potter's face cloud over.

"Not that kind of doctor," Candice whispered.

"Candice . . . " Mrs. Potter picked up her tea and emptied it into the sink. "Think carefully about this." Mrs. Potter walked out of the kitchen, leaving behind her a heavy silence.

"I will." Candice could feel Mrs. Potter's disappointment as if it were something tangible filling the room. If she chose to end the pregnancy, she was on her own. Sighing, Candice picked up her tea and walked back to her bedroom, her mind flipping between choices.

Have the baby; get rid of the baby. Tell Brad; keep quiet. Give her future away; disappoint Mrs. Potter.

If she chose to get rid of the baby . . . well, it *was* her body, after all. She shouldn't feel guilty about deciding what she could do with it. But then why did the thought of getting rid of this baby feel so *wrong?*

Candice shuddered. Mrs. Potter's more traditional beliefs must have rubbed off on her. Mrs. Potter always spoke to Candice about the sanctity of life, purity, and marriage; but after the fiasco that had been her parents' marriage, Candice didn't believe in the traditional approach anymore. Her parents' split had cured her of her "happily ever after" fantasies.

Perhaps Mrs. Potter's words did have some effect on her choices, though, because Candice had waited more than five months before she'd given herself to Brad. And that one night, one moment, one decision had a consequence that there was no way she could have possibly seen. Never in a million years did she think she'd be that girl. What would Felicia and Willow think if they found out she was pregnant? She shuddered at the thought.

No, she couldn't have this baby. She'd tell Brad; he would agree that she should get rid of it. Then she would, and . . . well, then there would be no need to worry about it. No need to think about it. Just nothing.

The appeal of nothingness called to Candice; then, her stomach churned, and she realized for the first time that there was something else in there, too.

Candice's mind changed sides more than a dozen times before the clock had ticked over to the next hour.

CHAPTER SIX

Candice had hoped that the internet would provide her some clarity, but when she typed the words "teen pregnancy" into the search engine, the flood of information only overloaded her brain and worsened her confusion. She shakily sipped the tea Mrs. Potter had made her, still warm from earlier, and opened another tab. This time, she typed in the words "abortion clinic."

She felt sicker with every result.

Nausea crawled up inside her, and she clamped her hand over her mouth, trying desperately to keep the tea inside her body. She closed the webpages and slammed the laptop shut.

Candice couldn't understand why she was struggling so much with this decision. The thing inside her wasn't even a baby; it was just a bunch of cells right now. Getting rid of a couple extra cells wasn't a big deal.

With this in mind, Candice dialed Brad's number.

He picked up on the third ring, his voice groggy from sleep. "Hey, babe, what's up?"

"Nothing much," Candice lied. "I just really need to see you this morning."

"Oh, okay. Do you want me to come and get you for school?"

"Yeah, I'd like that," she said, trying to keep the nervous quiver out of her voice. "I'll see you soon."

"Yeah, see you." He said the words briskly and hung up, leaving Candice to listen to the dial tone.

Why did it suddenly seem so strange that Brad hadn't said he loved her? He'd told her "I love you" that fateful night; it was the one and only time he'd said those words to her. Candice had assumed that once would be enough to allay her worries, but now she wondered how much he'd meant it. She'd said those words, too, and now . . . well, now, she wasn't sure about anything.

Candice sipped at her tea and went back to the kitchen, placing her cup into the sink and taking a few crackers from the cabinet. Mrs. Potter tottered around the house, tidying purposefully. She didn't look at Candice, and Candice was grateful she didn't say anything. Any decision she needed to make would be hard enough, and she could only hope that Brad would be on board, too.

Candice went through the motions of a typical morning, trying to pretend as if her reality hadn't been flipped upside down. She freshened up, styled her hair into a messy bun, and tried to recapture a semblance of normalcy. The ringing of a doorbell shattered her charade, and she felt nerves dance in her stomach as she opened the door.

Brad grabbed Candice close and kissed her with enthusiasm. After a moment, he pulled away and kicked the front door shut with his foot.

"Are we alone?" he asked kissing her again.

"Ah, no. Let's go to my room," she said.

"Your mom?"

"No, Mrs. Potter is here."

Brad smiled, pulling her close again and kissing her deeply. Candice knew she should pull away—this wasn't why she had asked to see him this morning. She needed to talk to him, but at this moment, Brad wasn't focused on words, and Candice didn't want to disappoint him. The news she was going to share would be disappointing enough.

So, when Brad began to pull her up the stairs, Candice let him. She didn't protest when he led them into her room, shut the door, and pulled her into another kiss. In fact, she kissed him back. Because she cared about him. Because she was terrified of losing him to Willow. Because this is what Willow would give him if Candice didn't.

Brad's hand slid from behind her back, and his fingertips skimmed over her stomach on his way further up her body.

I'm pregnant.

Candice froze, the thought dousing her body in ice. She pushed Brad away, and he stumbled back in surprise.

"Candice, what's going on with you?" Brad snapped.

"We need to talk." The air heaved in and out of her lungs. She had to be honest with him; she owed him that much. "I have something I need to tell you."

The seriousness of her statement must have penetrated his displeasure because his disgruntled expression became confused. "Okay . . . Should I be worried?" Brad grinned warily, hoping to lighten the atmosphere.

Candice sat down on the edge of her bed and took a deep breath. "Brad, do you remember that night at Felicia's party about two months ago?" The words came out garbled from her nerves, and she hoped Brad understood.

"The night Trent made a fool of himself?" he asked.

Candice sighed. Yeah, that had happened that night, too. "Do you remember what *else* happened that night?"

Brad watched her for a moment, and then the light went off. "Yeah, that was the night you and I, ah, you know . . . " His face colored slightly, and he swallowed.

Candice smiled. "Yeah. It was a special night."

Brad didn't do anything; he just stood there as if waiting for something. "You're really freaking me out, babe. What's going on?" He sat beside her, taking her shaking hands in between his.

She dropped her eyes to the floor. "I, ah . . . " She trailed off, shifting nervously on the bed. She squeezed his hands, still unable to meet his eyes.

"Candice." Brad tipped her chin up. "You can tell me anything, you know."

Was that the truth? She hoped so. It was now or never.

"I'm pregnant."

She whispered the terrible truth. Silence answered her.

She glanced up. Brad was staring at her, his face pale.

"Did you hear me?" she asked.

Brad pressed a fist to his mouth and began shaking his head back and forth, again and again.

Candice tried again, desperate for a response. "Brad, I'm pregnant, and you're the father."

He stared back at her. His blue eyes got wider and wider, his face paler and paler. His hands rigid and cold. It was as if her words had robbed all the warmth from his body.

"Brad?" He was scaring her.

Brad swallowed and stood, running an impatient hand through his hair and cracking his knuckles. Candice winced. Brad only did that when he was really disturbed about something.

"Brad, please . . . "

"Candice, I . . . " Brad stopped pacing and pulled her up, wrapping her into a hard hug. "It's okay."

The weight of a ten-ton truck lifted off of her, and she allowed herself to sag into Brad's embrace. "I thought . . . " Candice cleared her throat, swallowing back her anxiety.

"You thought?" Brad lifted her. "What did you think?"

"I thought you'd leave me." She hid her face in the shoulder of his sweater. Brad sighed and squeezed her tighter. His heart beat loudly in her ear.

"I'm not going anywhere," he said. Those were the best words she could have heard. "We got into this mess together, and we will get through it the same way."

Hope swelled within her, something she'd been too worried to wish for since taking the test. Brad was with her, and that was all that mattered. Brad kissed her quickly and sat them both down on the bed, still holding her in his arms.

"Are you okay?" he rested his chin on the crown of her head.

"Yeah. A bit sick but okay."

"The b-baby?" He stumbled around the word 'baby' like he was forcing himself to say something unpleasant.

Candice pulled back, watching Brad with renewed worry. "Brad?" His expression was slightly wild, the news of the past few minutes finally sinking in. His hands shook as they trailed up and down her back.

"Just give me a minute."

Candice fell silent, but the hope she had just felt was already beginning to wane. Brad's phone beeped in his pocket, but he ignored it, closing his arms tighter around her as they shook. For a long moment, they just sat.

"Brad, we're going to be late for school." Candice whispered, reluctant to move.

"Yeah, I know. If my dad finds out I skipped . . . " Brad trailed off with a shudder.

It wasn't the first time Brad had shown fear when speaking of his dad, and it wasn't the first time Candice worried about what went on in his home. She got off the bed and pulled Brad up with her.

"Give me a minute to get my stuff; then we can go," she said.

Brad nodded, his eyes wide and almost owl-like. He was stunned; but he had said he would be with her, and they would raise their baby together.

Their *baby.*

Candice ran an unsteady hand over her flat stomach. Was it really just a clump of cells? Or was it a baby—a *life?* And how did her answer to that question affect her decision? And would her decision change now that she had Brad by her side?

Together, they walked into the school, and Brad kissed her quick before hurrying to his science class.

"Hey, Candice! Why were you and Brad so late this morning?" Felicia swung around in her seat to look at her. There was a mischievous glint in her eye. "Playing hooky?"

Candice forced a laugh, wondering what Felicia and Amy would think of her and Brad's situation. And what would Willow think?

Well, if she found out, Willow wouldn't want anything to do with Brad, anyway. The anxiety over Brad and Willow disappeared as soon as that thought circulated. Brad was hers, and there was nothing Willow could do about it now.

"No, we just wanted to spend some time together before school," she said.

"Oh? Do tell." Felicia's smile turned wicked. "Just how much 'fun' did you two have this morning?"

"None of your business." Candice laughed genuinely this time, relieved that all would be well with her and Brad.

Mrs. Aria settled the class down.

"All right, let me quickly recap our lessons so far," she said. "As a baby grows inside the womb, it develops in stages from a single cell to a fully formed baby. By week two, the baby is an embryo; and at week four, the baby's features begin to form. At six weeks, with a good sonar, a baby's heartbeat can be heard. It is at the stage of eight weeks a baby is fully formed and continues to grow until the day of its birth."

Candice sucked in a sharp breath, thinking again about Brad. She ran her hand over her stomach again. There was a fully formed being inside of her.

Unease wormed up her spine as she watched Brad turn back to the front of the class. His expression was blank, and his back was rigid. When he glanced at her later, his kind expression from earlier was different—not mean, but distant.

Tension radiated off him. "Yeah. Just give me time, Candice. It's a huge shock, you know." He didn't lift his eyes up to hers as he walked away.

Candice bit her lip nervously and hurried to her next class. *He just needs time,* she told herself. Everything would be fine. They were in this together. But when Candice spent the next lunch period by herself in the bathroom, hunched over the toilet from nausea, she began to doubt that statement.

"Hey, are we still on for tonight?" Jack slid into the desk in front her like every other day. As if today didn't mark the end of Candice's life as she knew it. And as it was the end of her life as she knew it, she had totally forgotten about her plans to go to the basketball game with Jack.

"You forgot, didn't you?" Jack frowned.

"Yeah. I'm sorry," Candice said sheepishly. "But I'd still like to go! If that's okay?" Anything to take her mind off her current worries. Over the last week, Jack and Candice had grown closer as friends. He was kind, liked to laugh, and always seemed to know exactly what to say to make her feel better. And she wasn't failing math anymore, thanks to his help.

Jack's smile was somewhat appeased. "Of course. You look a bit pale, though. Are you feeling all right? Are you sure you wouldn't rather stay home?"

"No, I'll be fine. I'm just a bit tired." It wasn't a total lie; Candice hoped she'd get a few hours of sleep in between now and the game. The fiasco that morning had completely drained her.

"Great! Seven o' clock?" Jack held his hand out for a high-five, and she slapped her palm to his, her first true smile of the day inching its way onto her face.

Mr. Phillips' lesson passed by quickly, especially with Jack helping Candice through the tougher equations whenever he noticed her struggle. When they parted ways, Jack waved goodbye and walked quickly to his next class while Candice walked slowly to the student lounge. She had study period today. Mr. Van had given them their assignment yesterday and told them to spend the period in the student lounge working while he was away with the girls' volleyball team.

A loud giggle caught her attention as she walked past the gym; it was followed by a familiar chuckle. Normally, Candice would've ignored the sounds, but there was something about that laugh that stirred a memory. The gym was dark when she entered, but she heard the laughter again. This time, she could pinpoint that the sources were in the ball storage room at the back of the gym. The giggles were now interrupted with periods of suspicious silence.

Candice stepped closer; a sliver of light slipped through the crack between the doors. She placed her eye close to the crack, her heart beating rapidly until two people came into view.

It was Willow and Brad. Kissing.

Gasping, Candice covered her mouth with her hand and recoiled from the door. She shouldn't have worried about them hearing her though—they were so wrapped up in each other that she doubted they were aware of anything in the outside world.

Unable to handle the scene any longer, Candice rushed out of the gym, heartache slicing through her as she stumbled to the student lounge. The second bell had rung a long time ago, but she hadn't even noticed it. She sank into the couch and flipped open her laptop, desperate to distract herself with the day's lesson before she broke down in tears. She tried to push the image of Brad and Willow out of her mind. She'd been right about them, and something inside of her broke with that knowledge.

After her study period had ended and the final bell had rung, Candice struggled with her locker, the old combination lock sticking stubbornly.

Candice twisted the lock again—forward, backward, and around. She gave it a frustrated tug, blinking away angry tears and holding back a growl.

"Come on! Come *on*," she said, her tone filled with anger that wasn't really directed at the locker.

"Can I help?"

She whirled around, stomach fluttering as she came face to face with Jack's mirth-filled blue eyes. But then he caught sight of her flushed face and teary eyes, and his humored expression clouded over.

"Hey, are you okay?" The warmth of his hand seeped through her shirt sleeve as he guided her hand away from the lock.

Candice swallowed, trying to reign in her emotions. She refused to fall apart here.

"Yeah. I'm okay," she said, although, her words came out weaker than she had wanted. Jack frowned at her obvious lie. She decided to tell him part of the truth. "My lock is being particularly stubborn right now,"

"I noticed." Jack smiled and took the lock in hand. "Lucky for you, I just happen to be the master of all locks." He stepped back into an elaborate bow. "And I am at your humble service, madam."

Some of the suffocating grayness that hung over her lifted, and she giggled. "The combination is five-zero-one-three."

Jack shifted to get a better grip on her lock, and with a few quick twists, her locker sprung open.

"Ta-da!" He dropped into another bow and let out a bellow of laughter.

Sunshine. He was like much-needed sunshine after her rainy day, and Candice couldn't help her growing smile.

"Thank you, kind sir." She dropped into a playful curtsy.

Jack's fun-loving smile turned warm and hopeful. "So, are you still coming later?"

Candice considered her options. She could either go home and cry over a bowl of ice cream while huddled up in a fuzzy blanket, or she could spend some more time around the boy who had brought her a bit sunshine that day. It was an easy choice, especially when she saw his hopeful expression.

"Yes. But only because you rescued me from a locker disaster that was fraught with peril."

He beamed at her, radiating more sunshine. "Great! I'm looking forward to it."

His genuine excitement warmed Candice's heart, and her lips curled into a smile when he waved goodbye to her and walked out of the school into the afternoon sun.

The smile stayed on Candice's face while she grabbed the books from her locker and headed for the school exit. The hallways were nearly empty now. From the corner of her eye, she saw Willow and Brad walk hand-in-hand around the corner. Brad stiffened, his smile fading as he quickly dropped Willow's hand. He'd obviously expected the hallway to be empty as classes were well on their way.

Candice's heart clenched and she fought back her tears. Another silent scream caught in her throat. She wanted to rage, she wanted to ask him why. So, why wasn't she? Brad stood frozen in the hallway, his lips pressed together. Guilt swirled in those eyes she loved so much, swept across his face, and settled on his bobbing Adam's apple.

He was caught, and he knew it.

"Wait, Candice!" He made a move toward her; Willow held him back, her red-stained lips turned into a triumphant smile. Brad yanked his arm free from her and reached out to Candice again.

Candice wasn't waiting for the lies that would fall from his lips. Spinning on her heel, she turned and ran out of the school building to her car. She slammed the car door shut, cutting off the sound of Brad's desperate shouts. She glanced dry-eyed into her rear-view mirror as she drove away.

Mrs. Potter was right.

CHAPTER SEVEN

The gym was packed for the evening's basketball game. Candice walked to the concession stand, grabbing a hotdog and root beer before settling into her seat. Jack spotted her from across the room, and he quickly excused himself from his teammates to jog up to her.

"I was beginning to think you weren't coming." He looked so happy to see her that her heart lifted at the sight.

"Yeah, I had a rough day," Candice said vaguely. What an understatement. "I decided to take a nap and overslept a bit."

The truth was that she'd spent the evening staring at the ceiling and had fallen asleep two hours ago with her stomach in knots. The tears hadn't come, and she couldn't help but wonder why they hadn't.

"Well, I'm glad you decided to come," Jack said, shooting her a kind smile. Candice deeply appreciated that he didn't pry.

"I am, too." And she meant it.

"Hey, Jack!" The basketball coach, a tall man with a red Bethel Tiger's hat, beckoned him over, and a teasing grin snuck onto his face as he looked at the pair. "It's game time. You can flirt later!"

Candice stifled a laugh, watching Jack's ears flush red as he waved his coach off.

"I, uh, I'll see you after the game?" Jack scratched the back of his neck as if unsure about her response.

"Of course," she said. She couldn't help but smile—even though she knew the coach was just joking, she had to admit that Jack's flustered attitude was a bit endearing. "Good luck or whatever you say in this case."

"Good luck works just fine—better than 'break a leg.'" Jack looped his way back to his team's side of the court, giving his coach a quick smack on the arm as he went.

Candice settled into her seat and took a bite of the hotdog, the combination of ketchup and mustard lulling her to days long ago with her dad. She smiled as a fond memory of a camping trip came to mind. She'd been six, and her dad had planned a weekend at the lake. It had been a cool fall evening; the red and yellow leaves were piled in small heaps where her dad had cleared a space for their tent. She could still remember her parents laughing side by side in the warm light of the campfire, and in that moment, she'd thought her life was perfect.

Oh, how wrong she'd been.

The shrill sound of the whistle cut through her thoughts, yanking the memory away from her. Candice's focus returned to the game, back to a reality so far from that seemingly perfect past. The game had begun.

Jack was like a machine, and even for someone who knew nothing about basketball, Candice couldn't help but admire Jack's finesse. His hands always seemed to know just where the ball would be, his shots perfect as they whirled and bounced through the net. Candice sat in awe, totally entranced by the beauty of Jack's playing.

At the half, the Bethel Tigers led sixty-two to fifty. Excitement danced through Candice as Jack glanced her way, a wide smile lighting his face before he disappeared into the locker room with his teammates. The crowds cheered them in a loud chorus as they left. Electric excitement buzzed in the air.

"Hello! Could I sit here?" A tall woman with sandy blonde hair and warm, blue eyes asked, pointing to the blue bucket seat beside Candice.

"Of course," Candice said, gathering her trash quickly and moving it out of the way.

"Thank you! I'm running so late. I hope my son hasn't noticed my absence yet." The woman sat and looked down at the entrance to the locker room.

"Oh, I'm sure he'll understand," Candice said. "Which one is he?"

"Jack—he's the tall one coming this way," she said proudly.

Candice looked out onto the court to see Jack leaving the locker room. The woman stood with a huge smile, waving eagerly from the stands. Jack's smile grew to match his mom's, and he quickly ran toward them, taking the metal steps two by two.

"Mom, you made it," he said.

"I told you I'd try! I'm sorry I'm late, but at least I made it for the second half. The clinic was crazy today."

"I appreciate it. I know how busy your week has been." Jack turned to smile at Candice. "I see you've met Candice."

"Candice?"

"You know, the girl . . . " Jack sounded almost embarrassed as he gestured to her, his cheeks ruddy.

"Oh, *that* Candice." Jack's mother winked at him, making his blush grow even redder. "It's lovely to meet you. I'm Lily Anson."

Jack's mother took Candice's hand in hers and squeezed it gently. Together, they watched as Jack tossed them a wave and ran back toward his teammates. Lily's expression was something Candice doubted she'd ever see on her own mother's face. It was an expression of deep love and pride, and it made Candice's heart ache.

"So, how long have you known Jack?" Lily asked.

"Not long. I mean, we've been in the same math class all year, but Jack and I only got to know each other in the last week or so. I'm terrible at calculus, and—"

"And let me guess—Jack offered to tutor you?" Lily finished. Candice could've sworn that she was hiding a knowing smile under those tightly pressed lips.

"Yeah, he's been really kind to me," Candice said.

"Good! Then, I guess I did my job well," Lily said with a laugh. The sound was so contagious that despite the terrible day she'd had, Candice found herself laughing along. It seemed the Anson family's ability to spread happiness was an inherited trait.

At the end of the game, the Tigers emerged as the winners with a score of ninety to seventy-five, the last point from a swirling buzzer-beater. Jack let out a loud whoop as the ball sank into the net. Taking Candice by the hand, Lily hurried down to the courtside, dragging Candice behind her. Candice didn't mind; Lily's excitement and pleasure was contagious. As they reached courtside, Lily swept Jack into a big hug before releasing him.

"Well done, Son! Another win for the season. At this rate, you guys will be in the playoffs in no time."

"Stop, Mom!" Jack said. "You're making me blush." He ran his hand through his wet hair, his cheeks rosy.

Lily laughed and tapped him on the shoulder. "I guess that's my cue to say good night." She turned to face Candice. "Candice, it was lovely to meet you. I hope to see you again soon," she said with a wink.

Jack let out an awkward laugh and began to usher his mom away. "Good night, Mom! Love you." Jack hooked an arm around his mother's shoulders and turned her to the parking lot, whispering furtively into her ear. Lilly laughed and said louder, "I love you, too, Jack. Don't stay out too late, okay? It is a school night."

"Okay, Mom." Jack saluted his mother with a wide smile.

Suddenly, Lily turned back around and pulled Candice into a tight hug. Although she was shocked at first, Candice quickly melted into the embrace. She couldn't remember the last time her mother had hugged her. "It really was lovely to meet you, Candice."

With one last wave, Lily turned and walked out to the parking lot.

Jack shifted and settled his hands on his hips. His hair still glistened with sweat from the game. "Look," Jack began, sounding a bit unsure. "I know you have a boyfriend, but I was wondering if you'd like to come and grab some dinner with me. I'm starving, and I would hate to have to go alone. After I've had a shower, of course." He grimaced dramatically.

Candice grinned and was caught in his gentle gaze. At that moment, she considered telling him everything. *Calm down, Candice, you barely know this guy.* The night had been so good for her, and here in this moment, she felt like any other normal teenage girl. She just couldn't bear to ruin it.

"Okay," Candice said, sending a soft smile his way. "I'd like to go eat with you." Being out with Jack was a lot better than overthinking in an empty house.

"Really?" Jack's smile could have outshone the sun. "Great! Do you want to meet me at Denny's?"

Candice's heart dropped. Denny's had always been *their* place. Hers and Brad's. Was he there with Willow tonight?

She shifted awkwardly, pulling her shirt sleeves over her hands. "Maybe somewhere else?"

Jack frowned but nodded. "Ah, sure. I know this great pizza place near your house. What if I follow you home, and then we go together?"

"Sounds like a plan," Candice said, relieved. Jack smiled again and hurried to the locker room to shower. Candice let out a deep sigh and leaned against the brick wall nearby. Voices trailed down to her as the spectators to the game left in twos and threes. A young couple with a small child caught her gaze, and she grimaced. That would be her in a few months. She pushed all thoughts of Brad and the baby from her mind before they could send her into a spiral.

Soon enough, Jack strode from the locker room, freshly showered and dressed in a smile and casual sweats.

"Ready?"

"Yeah."

After a quick trip home, Candice climbed into Jack's red pickup truck. It was as neat as a pin and certainly cleaner than any other teenage boy's car she'd been in. Jack smirked as her eyes scanned the interior of the car.

"My mom is a nut for neatness. I guess it rubbed off on me." He shrugged and slid the car into drive. The engine hollered loudly as they drove away.

"What?" he asked when Candice stifled a giggle.

"Is this car a dinosaur or what?"

Jack let out a loud laugh that made Candice grin. "Yeah, it belonged to my dad," he said. "I love it, though. I mean, it's a real piece of history right here." Jack rubbed the dashboard affectionately. "Betty and I have traveled many miles together."

Candice didn't try and suppress her laughter this time.

"Betty?"

Jack flushed. "My grandma's name."

"I think it's cute."

Jack mumbled something unintelligible and shifted the car onto the road.

"Where to, my lady?"

"Well, I know you said pizza, but how would you feel about May's Bakery? I'm in the mood for a marshmallow chocolate float boat."

Jack wrinkled his nose. "Seriously? Do they even make food there?"

Another giggle bubbled up at Jack's disgusted expression. "Of course, they do. May has the best sub sandwiches on this side of the county. At least, that's what Mrs. Potter always says."

"Mrs. Potter?"

"My nanny-slash-mother-slash-housekeeper. She's the one who looks after me when . . . " Candice trailed off, emotion constricting her throat.

"When?" That concerned expression was back.

"Mrs. Potter looks after me more than my own mother has in a long time. A very long time," Candice admitted. Candice rarely talked to anyone about her family situation, but for some reason, Jack felt safe to her.

"I'm sorry, Candice." Jack said the words with such sincerity that a lump formed in her throat. A lone tear trickled down her cheek, and she wiped it away, hoping Jack hadn't noticed.

"It's okay," she said. "I guess I should be used it by now."

Jack reached over and gently took her hand. He watched her, waiting for her to pull her hand away. She didn't. It felt nice for someone to care. Her hand stayed in his as they drove into town, an old country song playing in the background.

May's Bakery was always busy, but tonight only the usual suspects were there.

"Good evening. Table for two, please," Jack said to the hostess, tugging Candice gently next to him, her hand still grasped tightly in his.

"My, my, if it ain't Miss Candice Hillman." A strong voice came from somewhere in the diner. A large woman with dark skin and a broad, inviting smile walked toward them and gathered them into a hard hug.

Candice blushed deep red, and Jack wore a bemused expression as the woman released them.

"Aunty Betty! It's been ages. How are you?" Candice studied the woman's large face, a memory lingering somewhere in the back of her mind.

"Yes, it has. I haven't seen you in years. Your Matilda still talks about you every time she comes in. And look how beautiful you are." Betty grasped Candice by the shoulder and studied her. Candice's cheeks burned brighter when she saw Jack grinning behind Betty, nodding his head enthusiastically.

"It's good to see you again, Aunt Betty. This is my friend Jack," Candice said, trying to divert attention away from her.

"My, my, he is a handsome one!" Aunt Betty said. Now it was Jack's turn to blush.

"It was good to see you, girl." Betty gave Jack another appraising look and, seemingly satisfied with what she saw, walked them to a nearby booth. "Come on, y'all. Nelly, bring these people some menus."

Jack sat next to Candice, and the two teenagers watched the large woman bustle around the room, directing the wait staff. A moment later, a middle-aged woman with a long, dark braid appeared beside their table.

"What can I get ya?" the waitress, Nelly, asked, handing them two cardstock menus. Jack flipped the menu over, took a quick glance, and laid it down again. "I'll have a coke and a meatball sub with extra fries." Candice swept her gaze over the menu, pleased to see they still had her favorite.

"I'll have a marshmallow chocolate float boat, please."

"Sure thing. Be back in a jiffy," Nelly said.

Jack settled back into his seat watching Candice. He seemed happy, and he really was handsome. The flush from Betty's earlier statement sprung back to life. Why was he watching her like that?

"So, tell me about 'Jack.' All I really know about you is that you are good at math and can play basketball like a pro," Candice said, trying to shift attention away from herself.

Jack laughed brightly. "I don't think I've ever received a nicer compliment."

"Yes, well, don't expect it all the time," she said playfully.

Jack chuckled and answered her earlier question. "Not much to tell. I'm the youngest of two. Older brother is named Trent; I'm sure you've heard of him."

Candice nodded. Trent and Felicia had somehow got tangled up in the past, but Candice wasn't sure what was between them now. "I have."

There was an uncomfortable silence. Thoughts of Felicia led to thoughts of Willow and Brad. Anger flashed like lightning through her, and she bit it back. Brad didn't deserve to ruin her nice evening, and Jack didn't deserve to have his evening ruined by Brad and his betrayal either.

Jack sighed and sat back in his seat. "Tell me about your dad."

"He's great. The best there is." A sudden sadness stole over her heart; her dad would be so disappointed with her. "I miss him."

Jack's hand reached across the table and enfolded her hand with his. "I'm sorry, Candice." Letting go, he sat back again, the picture of ease, while Candice's own emotions felt as if they were running a gamut. Brad, her dad, her mom, the baby—it was all too much.

"Do you plan on playing basketball after graduation?" she asked, grasping the first thing that came to mind.

Jack shrugged. "I'm not sure yet. I'm planning on college, and Coach says I will be able to get a scholarship, but honestly, I don't know what I want to do yet. Working with my hands and basketball are the only two things I love to do. You?"

She should have known he'd ask. Shrugging, she said, "I'm not sure either; maybe I'll go to college." Or maybe she'd have a baby and throw her life away.

"Well, I would love to know more about you," Jack said holding her gaze. "You know, like the deep stuff."

Candice's heart began to pound, her blood beating a deafening rhythm through her ears. "Deep stuff?" she asked.

"Sure, like, what's your favorite color, and do you like Coke or Pepsi? You know, the deep stuff."

Candice chuckled. "My favorite color is yellow, and I'm not a fan of either. I prefer tea or a chocolate milkshake."

Jack's eyes grew wide in mock surprise. "Seriously, no soda?"

"Nope."

Just then, Nelly arrived with their food, and Jack attacked his sub with gusto while Candice took a few bites of her dessert.

It was delicious, warm chocolatey goodness mixed with melted marshmallow and chunks of chocolate and graham crackers.

They ate in companionable silence until Jack took a long drink of his Coke and rubbed his stomach appreciatively. "That was delicious. I'm glad you talked me into coming here."

"Speaking of the deep stuff, what did you want to be when you were in the first grade?" Jack asked as he sipped his soda.

"In first grade . . . " Candice took another bite of ice cream, savoring the creamy flavor. "I wanted to be an archeologist, or at least some one who dug up dinosaur bones. My dad and I found a bunch of fish-shaped fossils in the backyard and some arrowheads. I was so excited that a few days later, my dad let me skip school and took me to the museum. Just me and him." Her heart panged again. She really missed her dad and the time they'd spent together when she was young. "What about you?"

"At the risk of sounding like a total cliché, I wanted to be an astronaut. My kindergarten teacher, Mrs. Paisley, took us to the planetarium, and that decided it for me. I was going to explore the great unknown of space." He grinned. "'Houston, we have a problem,'" he said in a rough, comical voice.

Candice chuckled and took another bite. Jack emptied his glass and signalled Nelly for a refill.

Remembering a good joke she'd heard, she said, "You know, I saw Mr. Phillips with a piece of grid paper yesterday . . . "

Jack looked confused. "Yeah, he's always got something like that with him."

Candice deadpanned her expression. "I think he's plotting something."

Jack's eyebrow lifted to his forehead before his laughter bellowed out around the diner. It was so infectious that Candice couldn't help joining in.

When their giggles subsided, Jack leaned his forearms on the table. "That was great. Okay, I've got one for you. Why is math class always so long?"

"Because Mr. Phillips likes to talk?" Candice answered.

"No, because he always goes off on a tangent."

Candice laughed so hard, her sides ached. "Okay, bad math jokes aside, if there was anywhere in the world you could go, where would it be?"

"The NBA finals," Jack said, grinning widely.

"Seriously?"

"No, but it is on my bucket list. If there was somewhere in the world I could go, it would probably be to Alaska."

"Alaska? Why there?"

"It's kind of like a coming-of-age trip. My grandfather went when he was my age; he said it was an amazing experience that taught him how to be the man he was." Jack's smile turned wistful. "My grandfather was a great man."

"Where is he now?"

Candice didn't know her grandparents. Her mother had grown up in foster care, and her father's parents lived in Jamaica. Candice had seen them for the first and only time when she was four years old.

"Grandpa passed a year ago. Gran is still alive and kicking, the feisty, old lady."

An unfamiliar sadness joined her mess of emotions. What was it like to have a family that was so close?

"Is there anything else I can get ya?" Nelly asked, menus in hand again.

Jack glanced at Candice, and she shook her head. "No, thank you. I think we're ready for the bill," he said.

Candice reached for her purse and withdrew her wallet.

"I got it," Jack said and handed Nelly his card to pay for the food. Candice knew it was the gentlemanly thing to do, but they weren't on a date. Jack didn't need to pay.

"Jack," she protested.

Jack shook his head. "It's done. My mama raised me right." It sounded like there was a double meaning to his words, and she wondered at them.

Becoming familiar with his stubborn look, she shrugged and closed her purse, wallet inside. "Thank you."

When the bill was settled, they said goodbye to Betty and Nelly and walked toward the car. Jack didn't take her hand again, and she missed the comfort of his touch.

"I had a really nice time tonight, Candice. Thank you for coming with me." Sincerity bled into his every word and warmed her heart. He put the gearshift in park outside her house.

"I had a nice time, too. Even with the bad jokes," Candice said, a small smile on her lips.

Jack chuckled again. "I'll see you in the morning?"

Candice nodded. "See you in the morning." She climbed out of the car, waving as Jack pulled out from the drive.

After Jack dropped her off, Candice slipped back into her house, exhaustion hanging on her. The betrayal and sorrow she had managed to ignore all evening was beginning to suffocate her happiness. She took one step after another into the dark silence of her house. She wished her mother was home, but as it was, the garage was empty.

Pulling out her phone, she dialed her father's number.

"Candice? Are you okay?" her father answered. His voice was heavy with sleep.

"Yeah, Daddy. Sorry I woke you up; I just wanted to hear your voice," Candice said.

"Oh, my girl. Are you okay?" he asked, sounding more alert.

"I don't know," Candice said honestly. "A boy broke my heart." She sniffled. She wasn't ready to tell her dad about the pregnancy. She didn't want him to abandon her, too.

"Oh, Candice, I'm sorry. Don't you worry, I'll be right over with my shotgun," he said.

Candice snorted. As helpful as her father wanted to be, Westwood was over five hours away, and it was the middle of the night.

"It's okay, Daddy. I should have seen it coming." A few more tears slid down her cheeks.

"I wish I was there to give you a hug," he said sadly.

"That's all right. We're still on for this weekend, right? You'll be here tomorrow at four?" she asked.

"Yes. Right after I hunt down that boy for breaking your heart."

A tearful laugh escaped her. Her dad, Damon Hillman, was always wanting to slay her dragons. "I'll be okay, Dad. I'll see you this weekend," she said.

"Goodnight, Candice. I love you."

"I love you, too, Dad."

With a click, the phone went quiet, and the tears began to trickle down her cheeks. At least, her dad loved her. She would tell her father about the baby but perhaps not this weekend.

CHAPTER EIGHT

"Candice, I'm sorry." Brad stood on her porch, hands twisted in his hair, and his bloodshot eyes filled with guilt. It's a wonder his incessant knocking and hollering hadn't woken the whole neighborhood or Mrs. Potter in her bed in the pool house.

Candice glanced at the dark sky, wiping her puffy eyes with the sleeve of her pajamas. "Brad, what are you doing here? It's five in the morning."

"I know. I've been outside your house since two. Can I come in?" he asked desperately.

Stepping aside, Candice swung to door open wider. "Fine."

Brad followed her into the living room, but when he made a move to sit beside her on the sofa, she put her hand up to stop him. Sighing loudly, Brad sat on the loveseat opposite her.

"Candice, I'm so sorry," he said. His hands fidgeted with his messy hair. "I didn't mean for this to happen. With Willow and the baby and . . . "

"How long?" she asked.

He swallowed, clearly uncomfortable. "For about three weeks . . . "

Candice's heart dropped. "So, when I told you about the baby, you were planning on leaving me, anyway?"

"No! That day, I had decided to end it with Willow, but then she came to my house and . . . " he trailed off.

Candice could only imagine what had happened next. Bile crawled up her throat. "Stop. I don't need to know the rest."

Brad nodded, color flooding his cheeks and ears. It used to be cute, but now it smacked with betrayal.

"I'm sorry. I never meant for it to happen," he said, sighing heavily.

"Then why did it?"

Brad dropped his head into his hands. "I don't know. Willow is impossible to resist."

Anger burning through her, Candice rose to her feet. Her body ached, and the sickness she'd felt in previous mornings creeped into her throat. She was furious and hurt and absolutely disgusted.

"You should go," she said. She grabbed Brad by the arm and began to pull him toward the door.

"But—"

"Now, Brad," she gasped, desperately swallowing back the nausea and fighting back the tears.

She swung the door open and pushed Brad outside. He turned to stare at her, his eyes wide and guilt-ridden. She couldn't look at him. Those eyes had lied to her too many times.

"I'm sorry, Candice. I—"

Candice slammed the door shut, locked it, and ran for the nearest bathroom, crying softly.

The pain from the early morning conversation with Brad hung heavily on her shoulders as she drove to school. After spending over two hours desperately debating with herself and then with Mrs. Potter, she'd made a decision: the only way to save herself and the baby from the betrayal she now felt was to make sure they'd never have to face the same pain and devastation. She had been discarded by her mother and abandoned by Brad, and if her father ever found out about the pregnancy, he'd surely leave her, too.

The only way to protect herself was to stop the pregnancy, and by doing so, she'd spare the baby a future of pain and abandonment, too.

What about Mrs. Potter? The little voice returned to her head. Mrs. Potter would probably never speak to her again after the decision she'd made today. No, Mrs. Potter was as good as gone now, too.

And you're going to spare your baby from abandonment by abandoning them, too? The voice asked. Candice cringed. It was different. She was being proactive. She was protecting the baby—the unborn child would never know any different.

Candice tried to convince herself of this twisted logic, but even so, the weight on her shoulders only grew heavier with every counterargument.

Blinking back her tears, Candice parked her car and took a few minutes to gather her thoughts. Then, the car door swung open.

"Is it true?" Felicia asked, standing outside the car.

"Is what true?" Candice asked. She was exhausted.

"You and Brad?" Her eyebrow rose suggestively. She had to be talking about that night. It wasn't a secret what went on a Felicia's parties; everyone knew where you were going when you disappeared into a room together.

"Come on, Felicia. You know that's old news."

Felicia rolled her eyes. "Not that. The rumor that you and Brad are . . . you know. Are you?"

"Come on, just spit it out. My brain is too tired to run around now. Am I what?" But as soon as the words were out, realization dawned on Candice. Her palms began to sweat. He wouldn't have told people. He wouldn't do that to her.

"Are you pregnant?"

He had. Shame filled Candice. Tears rushed into her eyes, and then she felt warm all over. If it were possible for lava to run through a person's veins, she was sure it felt like this. Her silence must have been answer enough because Felicia bent down beside her and hugged her fiercely.

"Oh, Candice. I'm so sorry."

Clearing her throat roughly, Candice looked into Felicia's blue eyes. "How did you find out?"

"I think the better question is how did Willow find out? I just got here and heard her talking about it. Do you think Brad told her?" A loud peal of laughter echoed around the busy school yard. Felicia met her gaze; they both knew who was to blame.

"Willow." Felicia nodded, and an expression that Candice had never seen crossed Felicia's brown skin. It was an expression of fury.

"Let me guess—after she stole Brad, she spread the news." Felicia sighed. "I'm sorry."

"How could he do this to me?" Candice asked, burying her face in her hands. "He apologizes this morning and then does *this*?"

Felicia shook her head and rubbed Candice's back. Eventually, Candice composed herself enough to walk into the school, Felicia at her side.

Silence greeted Candice when she entered the school building. She could feel eyes judging her from every direction, and low whispers following her every footstep. Stiffening her spine, Candice straightened her shoulders and walked with her head high, refusing to cower before the crowd. Amy and Willow stood outside of their first class, whispering furiously behind their hands. Felicia nodded at Candice and shot her an encouraging smile as she walked off toward her own class, leaving Candice to make a decision. To ignore or confront?

A dark sense of foreboding shadowed Candice as she approached Willow and Amy.

"Willow. Amy," she said curtly.

Willow's beautiful face transformed, her smiled vanishing and a sardonic sneer replacing it. "Candice."

It still amazed Candice how Willow could fool people with her beauty; she was nothing but a snake dressed up in a beautiful smile.

"I won," Willow said simply. An ugly smile bent her lips. "Come on, Amy. We have no more business here."

Any idea Candice had of standing up for herself vanished at Willow's chilling giggle. Brushing Candice off, Willow flounced into the classroom with Amy following her like a sheep.

A lonely tear slipped down Candice's cheek. Any lingering doubt she had about her earlier decision was whisked away—she was going to stop the pregnancy, pretend it was all some fake rumor that Willow started, and restart her life as normal.

Squeezing her eyes shut, Candice fought back her tears and walked into class, deliberately ignoring the guilt-filled expression that Brad shot at her from across the room. From the front of the room, Mrs. Aria droned on and on about the incredible responsibility of being a parent, and she pleaded with those who were unfortunate enough to find themselves in that position to stay strong and make the right decision, which, according to her, was to keep the baby. *Be responsible.*

Brad walked past the doorway, his gaze fixed on her. Candice glared back until he cowered back to his own class, then she hunched deeper into her chair. No doubt Mrs. Aria had heard the rumors, too. Was it just her imagination, or did her sympathetic eyes pass over Candice again and again?

Eventually, the bell rang, and Candice grabbed her bag. She needed to leave—needed to go anywhere but here.

"Candice?" Her heart lurched at the sound of his voice.

"Go away, Brad," she whispered.

"Can we talk, please?" he said.

"I think we've spoken enough. Don't you? You certainly spoke to Willow enough," she said bitterly, turning to face him.

Anger filled Brad's eyes, the soft blue she'd become accustomed to turning into flint.

"What are you going to do?" he asked.

Anger flared within her. How *dare* he ask about their baby when he'd already chosen to abandon them?

"How is that any of your business?"

He was silent for a moment, the frustration in his eyes turning pained. "Are you going to get rid of it?" he asked.

"I don't see how that's your problem. After all, what do you care? Scared Willow's gonna dump you?"

His expression hardened. "No. I'm not ready to be saddled with a baby now. I just got a full-ride football scholarship."

Candice recoiled. Once again, he was only worried about himself. "Well, in that case, don't worry, Brad. Whatever I decide to do no longer concerns you."

She left him behind and hurried toward the library, the weight of her sorrow almost suffocating her. She swung the library doors open and slipped into an aisle between the bookshelves, her blood thundering through her veins. Sinking to the floor, she surrendered to her pain, the dim light between the shelves giving her the privacy she craved.

The pain came, wave after wave pulling her into its murky depths. Brad's attitude and his indifference had hurt her more than he could imagine. Her isolation formed a wrecking ball that destroyed any semblance of calm and hope she might have once felt. This was it. Life was over, and she knew without a doubt that she was forever changed. Bitterness seeped like poison into her veins, followed quickly by anger that built into rage.

Just when she thought the aching emotion would swallow her whole, she heard a voice bring her back from the brink.

"Candice? Are you in here?"

Jack.

Candice put a hand over her mouth to muffle her sobs. Jack? What on earth was Jack doing here? Shouldn't he have been in class? Candice wiped away the mess of mascara under her eyes and stood. She was about to retreat deeper into the shadows of the bookshelves when she saw him. Jack rounded the corner and froze at the sight of her.

"Candice . . . " The horror in Jack's expression only fed the desperation she felt, and the tears sprang freely from her again.

In seconds, Candice found herself cradled firmly against a warm chest, strong arms encircling her. She shouldn't let him—he wasn't hers. He didn't know the reason for her tears, but there was no one else to lean on.

"It's okay," Jack whispered. He held her quietly, rubbing her back until her tears were spent, and then together, they sat down in her dark alcove.

"What happened?" he asked. "On my way to the office, I heard Brad call you something that a polite gentlemen should never repeat."

Candice sniffed. She could guess what Brad said. Every time she tried to talk, more tears appeared. So, she stopped trying. She just shook her head and buried her face against his chest.

Jack sighed and wrapped his arms tighter around her shoulders. The bell rang, signaling the beginning of class. Candice pushed Jack away.

"You need to get to class," she said, voice thick with emotion. She tried to clear her throat. "I don't want you to get detention because of me."

"Nah, don't worry about it. Principal Rory owes me one." The dim light of the lamps glistened softy on his tawny hair; his eyes were dark, and his smile was sad. "What can I do to help?" His touch was so gentle and soothing. Candice gathered her shattered heart and tattered emotions.

"Come with me to the office?" She phrased it as a question so Jack would know that she was giving him a choice. He could leave her, too, if he wanted. Like everyone else. She wouldn't force him.

"Sure." There wasn't a moment's hesitation in his answer, and Candice suddenly felt like she could breathe a little easier.

Jack stood and swung her bag onto his right shoulder, his left arm coming around her shoulders as he led her to the library doors. The hallway was deserted, and they walked in companionable silence to the office. Once they reached the office, Jack returned her bag, offered her a gentle smile, and handed her a small piece of paper from his pocket.

"I couldn't think of a good time to give this to you," he said. "But if you need anything, send me a text." Jack gave a playful bow and ran down the hallway, presumably to his next class.

Candice stared down at the paper, examining the hastily scrawled numbers with a small smile. After a moment, Candice took a deep breath and swung open the office door, coming face to face with Mrs. Fredericks.

Mrs. Fredericks nodded at Candice. "You look like you've been through the ringer, honey. I'll send Mrs. Potter a message to expect you."

Gratitude left her speechless, and she nodded her thanks, willing her tears not to fall.

CHAPTER NINE

Just when she thought she couldn't handle any more emotional stress, Candice's mother appeared.

She came out of the kitchen, impeccably dressed, as soon as Candice slammed the front door shut. Andrea Hillman. Candice carried a lot of her in her looks. They shared the same burned auburn hair, high cheek bones, and pointed nose. Candice's eyes came from her father.

"Mom? What are you doing here?" Candice asked, surprised by her sudden appearance.

Her mother must have come back to pack for another trip. That was the only reason she ever came home this early in the day.

"Me? Why aren't you at school?" her mother asked.

"I didn't feel well," Candice answered vaguely. She composed herself, slinging her backpack over her shoulder and purposefully turning her face where her mother couldn't see it.

"Candice?" The shrill tone of her mother's voice grated on Candice's already frazzled nerves. Her mother's voice always took on that tone when Candice said something flippant. It used to frustrate her when her mother used that tone; but today, Candice was emotionally spent, and she just couldn't make herself care.

"I'm going upstairs," she said.

Mrs. Potter stood in Candice's view, disapproval pouring off her. Her deep brown eyes begged Candice to reconsider.

Not today. She didn't have it in her.

Candice turned her eyes away, stiffened her spine, and marched up to her room. If her mother wanted to speak to her, she could come and find her.

The pale blue walls and yellow, daisy-patterned curtains in her room greeted Candice with the first bit of sunshine she'd seen all day. Daisies were her favorite flower; they reminded her of better times, like spring days and lazy afternoons on a canoe with her dad. Today, she missed those days more than ever.

Candice sank down under her covers, shielding her eyes from the persistent light of the afternoon sun. She sighed when she heard a car door close and an engine start—Mom was on her way off again. Figures.

What was Candice going to do? The simple answer hung like a noose teasing her. The only way life would go back to normal was to make it normal again. Her resolve hardened like concrete. She had work to do. Candice pulled out her laptop and settled it onto her knees. The screen was still blank when her father called her later. She still didn't tell him she was pregnant. What her dad didn't know couldn't hurt him.

"Hey, you." Jack said, smiling at Candice when she walked into math class. "You ready for some serious summing today?"

Candice laughed lightly. Today, the world looked brighter. "Yeah, actually, I wanted to ask you something."

"Yeah?"

"Is your offer to tutor me still good? As you've noticed, I'm kind of bad at this."

Jack chuckled. "Believe me, I've noticed. I'd be happy to. How does this afternoon sound?"

"Sounds great!" Candice beamed. Jack gazed back at her, looking happy to see a smile had returned to her face.

Mr. Phillips brought the class to attention and introduced the next lesson. Candice sighed and glanced over at Jack, who worked vigorously at the desk beside her. He looked up and winked, and her heart thumped heavily. When had he become so good-looking to her?

Shaking her head at the intrusive thoughts, Candice turned her attention back to her work and waited for the bell to ring.

"Are you going to tell me why you were crying yesterday?" It was after school, and Jack and Candice were at the library. For about an hour, they had puzzled over the last month's math problems. Jack was a fantastic teacher and more patient with her than Brad had ever been.

"If you don't mind, I just want to concentrate on math right now," Candice said, gripping her pencil a bit tighter.

Jack must've heard the rumors. But why hadn't he asked her about them? Maybe he didn't listen to school gossip—after all, there were more lies than truth in the hallways. And maybe the stars would align, and her life would be perfect again. Yeah, there was a fat chance of that happening. Everybody heard and listened to rumors. So, why hadn't he asked?

Jack gazed at her quizzically for a moment. Apprehension grew in her stomach.

"So . . . I heard a rumor today," he began carefully. Her stomach dropped. "About you and Brad. Feel free to tell me to mind my own business at any point."

"Look, Jack. We—"

"Did you break up?" he asked.

Wait . . . Was that what he was really asking?

Relief lifted the heavy weight from her shoulders. "Yeah. Willow got her claws into him."

Strangely, saying the words out loud didn't hurt nearly as much as she thought they would. She'd thought she was in love with Brad, and now . . . well, now she knew better. What she and Brad had wasn't love, and she regretted not seeing it sooner.

"I'm sorry. Is that the reason you weren't with your usual crowd at lunch?" Jack turned back to his textbook and opened to the next section.

"Yes." Well, it was *part* of the reason.

The muscle in Jack's jaw twitched as if he was considering something and then decided against it. "Okay."

Did she approach the elephant in the room? Even if she was the only one who could see it? Jack smiled at her. No. Maybe he didn't need to know. By next week, there would be nothing to talk about.

"Can I ask you a question now?" she asked.

"Sure." Jack shrugged.

"Why did you offer to tutor me?"

Jack flushed. "Actually, for two reasons. First, you're really bad at math. Second, like I told you at the diner, I want to get to know you— you know, the deep stuff," he said with a wink. He was teasing her.

Candice ducked her head. "You shouldn't. You don't want to be my friend, Jack." She was too messed up for someone with a good heart like Jack.

"But I do. I want to be your friend. I noticed you seem to be lacking those right now." Jack gestured to the empty room around them.

"I don't think I would make a very good friend to you, Jack." The secret she bore would kill any chance of her and Jack being friends or anything else. She wouldn't drag Jack down into the muck with her, not after he'd been so sweet.

"Why don't you let me be the judge of that?" Jack crossed his arms over his chest and leaned back in his chair.

Candice hesitated, looking up at Jack's welcoming face and soft smile. And she couldn't help but give in. "Okay," she surrendered.

Silence hung between them as she stared at him, time ceasing. Jack abruptly cleared his throat, his cheeks flushed. A tiny grin lifted his lips. "Let's look at the next section. I know this will be in the test."

"Okay, hit me with it," Candice said, trying to get back into study mode. "I understand the formula, but when you add the table, I can't seem to place the right values."

"It's simple. Here, I'll show you." Jack leaned a little closer pointing to the textbook. The smell of his warm cedar aftershave filled her senses and drew her attention far away from studying.

"Candice, did you hear me?"

"Yeah, sorry. Daydreaming," she said, blushing slightly.

"Okay, now . . ."

After about fifteen minutes of Jack's tutoring, Candice's head ached, but she had a better understanding of her course work. Jack shut the textbook with a loud bang.

"Okay, time for a break. What do you do for fun?" Jack asked.

"Fun?"

"Yeah, you know, the thing you do when you aren't doing this?" Jack gestured to the books heaped between them.

"Funny." She supposed she deserved that as distracted as she was. "Hang out, go shopping. Do you do anything besides tutor math and play basketball?"

"I help my mom at the center. You know, with heavy lifting and so on." Jack impishly flexed his muscles and grinned. Candice laughed.

"Center?"

"My mom works at the Save a Life Center in town. She helps teenage girls who are pregnant find good people to adopt their babies. She also counsels girls who have been abused."

Candice's stomach clenched. He couldn't know. Could he?

Jack tapped his pencil on the textbook. "What do your parents do?"

"My dad is an engineer, and my mother works at a publishing company. She's like an author babysitter or something. I don't actually know what she does,"

"Is that the reason she's never home?"

"Yeah, her clients are apparently more important than her child." The bitterness she felt toward her mother seeped into her words.

"I'm sorry, Candice." Jack frowned. "So, how does Mrs. Potter fit into this picture?"

Candice smiled at the thought of the woman. "My mom hired Mrs. Potter when we moved to Bethel. Mom started working more and more, and pretty soon, it was just me and Mrs. Potter. It's strange though—the divorce took me by surprise. My parents never talk about it, and to this day, I still don't know why they divorced."

"Where does your dad live now?"

"He still lives in our old house. I see him as often as possible." She really needed to tell her dad about the baby.

Jack nodded. "Sounds like you have a lot going on."

"Yeah, but that's life, isn't it?"

"Any brothers or sisters?"

"No. Only me. What does Trent do?"

"He's away at college. I think he drives my parents crazy, changing his major every semester. The latest is 'birds.' Honestly, who studies Ornithology?" Jack screwed his face comically. "If you asked my mom, though, she would tell you she has three sons: me, Trent, and Christian, my best friend."

Candice blinked. "So, if he's your best friend, then why aren't you hanging out with him instead of sitting in a library with me?"

"He's busy with something. Besides, you desperately needed my help, remember?" Jack teased. "Anyway, I was wondering . . . can I get your number?" Jack held his phone out to her suddenly, his Contacts app already open. "Just in case I get lonely on the way home tonight. You know how I love to talk."

Candice couldn't help the giggle that escaped her. "That's the cheesiest line I've ever heard." Still, she took the phone and typed in her information.

"Yeah, but it made you laugh, and I got your number. Mission accomplished!"

Jack took the phone back and typed something onto the screen. Candice's phone pinged with a new message:

Unknown Number: *Hi Candice!*

"Really? 'Hi Candice' is the best you've got?" Candice held her phone up to Jack.

"You know it." He grinned cheekily. "I wasted my good line earlier."

An hour later, Jack waved goodbye to her from his old, red pickup truck. Candice took a deep breath of cool air, relishing in the lingering happiness she felt. The sun was setting, and the darkness of the night already creeped over the town. She threw her bag into the passenger seat of her SUV and slid into the driver's seat. In the absence of Jack's company, the weight of the day was already beginning to stifle the little joy she had.

Jack drove home, his mind wandering again and again to his time spent with Candice. She was so different than he'd expected her to be. When they'd met that first day, he had assumed he would be dealing with another stuck-up princess like Willow, but he'd been wrong. So wrong. Where Willow was cold and calculating, Candice was warm and innocent. The way her eyes lit up with love when she spoke about Mrs. Potter and her dad showed she genuinely cared for people. And then there was the devastation of Brad's betrayal. Candice had a soft heart, and Brad's decision had hurt her deeply. And what of the rumors he'd heard? Were they true? Surely, she would have said something when they were together?

Slow your roll, Jack. She barely knows you.

That was true, too. Maybe if Candice could trust him, she'd talk to him about the rumors. Or maybe when they knew each other better, he would ask her about them. He shook his head; rumors were rarely true.

He pulled his car to a stop outside his house and swiped open his phone. He pulled up Candice's number as he walked to the back of the house and into his room.

Jack: *What did the one cheese say to the other one? You melt my heart.*

Candice: *Smooth, Casanova.*

Jack smiled and took a deep breath. If he wanted to get to know her better, it was time to take the plunge.

Jack: *Can I pick you up for school tomorrow?*

There was a long pause. Jack started to get nervous. Had he been too forward? Then, finally, his phone chimed.

Candice: *I'd like that.*

Jack sighed and flopped back onto his bed, Candice's face filling his vision. He *really* liked her.

But what about the rumors?

Only silence answered his busy thoughts, and he knew he wouldn't be able to decide tonight. His brain power was better spent on his mountain of homework. Reluctantly, Jack pulled out his physics book, his brain flip-flopping between the work in front of him and the potential that tomorrow could bring.

CHAPTER TEN

Tuesday morning, Candice pulled herself off the bathroom floor and into the shower. The queasiness in her stomach swirled as she flicked on the hot tap. The warm water eased some of the sickness, and a few quick sips of Mrs. Potter's ginger tea did the rest. Feeling better and ready for the day, Candice hurried down the stairs just as the doorbell rang.

"Who could be visiting at this hour?" Mrs. Potter asked, wiping her flour-covered hands on her apron.

"Just a friend," Candice answered. With shaking hands, she swung open the large wooden door.

Jack stood tall and gorgeous in front of her. His smile slid wider when he saw her.

"Good morning, fair lady." He made an elaborate bow.

"Good morning," Candice said with a laugh.

"Are you ready to go?"

"Yes! Let me grab my bag, and I'll be right out. I'll meet you at the car."

Jack nodded happily. "Okay." He turned and waltzed back down to his truck, leaning against the hood. She could feel his eyes on her. There were butterflies doing a frenzied dance in her stomach.

"Something you want to tell me?" Mrs. Potter tapped her on the shoulder, and her kind smile told Candice that it was a "mom" question. She was worried. The slight gleam in Mrs. Potter's eye told her that there would be more questions later.

"It's not what you think," Candice slid her backpack onto her shoulder. "He's just a friend who's helping me with math."

Mrs. Potter nodded, unconvinced. "Here." She handed Candice a cheese and ham sandwich, "You'd better go."

On impulse, Candice dropped her bag and threw her arms around her nanny. "Thanks, Mrs. Potter." She grabbed her bag and the sandwich, which had gotten a bit crushed in her enthusiasm, and ran out the door. Her eyes watered a bit as she rushed out the door; she was truly grateful to have Mrs. Potter in her life.

"Are you okay?" Jack asked, looking a bit worried for her.

"Yeah, I'm all right. Just grateful," Candice said.

A warm hand covered hers and squeezed gently. Her breath caught in her throat.

"Jack . . ."

"No hand-holding?" An easy smile rested on his lips.

Candice smiled, relieved. "I didn't say that. It's just . . ." Did Jack have feelings for her? His actions certainly showed he did, but how did she feel? It was too soon to know, but it was still nice to hold his hand.

Jack's smile grew when Candice reached over and laid her hand on his. Warmth filled her cheeks.

"Don't worry," he said. "Seriously, there are no expectations here. I just want to be your friend." He gave her hand another affectionate squeeze and laid it gently back in her lap.

Happiness fizzled through her, with a bit of caution mixed in. Was she doing the right thing by keeping her pregnancy from him? If it was that much of an issue, why didn't he just ask her about it? *Why don't you just tell him?*

The muscles at the base of his skull tensed as Jack brought the car to a stop outside the school. Brad, Willow, and their crew were gathered by the entrance, and all turned to watch him climb out of the truck and walk to the other side. He opened the door and helped Candice get out, keeping close to her side as they walked toward the group. His protective instincts went on full alert when Brad detached himself from the group and walked over to them. Candice stepped closer to Jack, and had the circumstances been different, it would have made him smile. Still, he felt touched by her trust in him.

"Hey, Candice. Slumming it, I see?" Brad crossed his muscled arms over his chest and glared at Jack. Jack wasn't sure how things had ended between them, but he knew it hadn't ended well. Was Brad jealous? The word around the school was Candice had found out Brad was messing around with Willow. He'd wanted to ask her about it the night before; but she had seemed happy, and he hadn't wanted to spoil her good mood.

"You have a problem, Brad?" Jack moved Candice behind him and stepped closer to Brad. He could take Brad, and Brad knew it. And he would if it meant protecting Candice from whatever hurt Brad had planned.

Brad faltered and his eyebrows shot into his hairline. He hadn't expected Jack to actually challenge him. A sneer curled his lips. "Don't go down this road, Jack. Haven't you heard the rumors?"

He had. He wondered about them day after day, but it never seemed like the right time to ask Candice about them. Whatever the truth was, he was willing to wait for Candice to tell him.

The shrill ringing of the bell interrupted any further discussion.

"So, I'll see you at lunch?" Jack pulled Candice into the flow of traffic going to class and gently pushed her on her way. He heard Brad scoff behind him and storm off. Good riddance.

"Sure." Candice's wide brown eyes gazed back at him. She looked scared, and he wished they had the time to discuss this now. But the second bell was seconds away from ringing; and if they were late, they would both be in trouble.

He took her cold hand, rubbing warmth into her delicate fingers. "Hey, don't listen to him. He isn't known for being anything other than a jerk." Her expression dropped, and tears filled her eyes as she nodded. Anger burned in his chest, but he tried his best to contain it.

Silently, they parted ways. Jack's heart ached for the pain Candice was going through. He turned and walked after Brad. It was time for a reckoning.

"What was that about, Thorn?" Jack said. He grabbed Brad's shoulder and spun him around to face him.

"None of your business, Anson. Move along," Brad said, shoving Jack's hand off his shoulder.

The flame turned white hot. "If it comes to Candice, I'm making it my business."

Brad barked a scornful laugh. "Good luck with that." Jack clenched his fists ready to pound Brad's face in. He readied himself. Surprise stopped him, though, when the arrogance and anger dissolved on Brad's face, and for just a moment, pain filled his eyes. "Just . . . Look after her, okay?"

Brad hung his head, shoulders slumped in defeat. Jack's anger left and resolve took its place.

"I will," he said. It was a promise Jack would gladly keep.

CHAPTER ELEVEN

Brad's eyes burned into her back as she entered Mrs. Aria's classroom. Why was he looking at her like that? After the vitriol he'd spewed at her before class, he should be giving her a wide berth. She opened her human development textbook and immersed herself in the information, oddly desperate to know what was going on with her body and what was growing inside of her. She ignored the sensation of being watched; she had nothing more to say to Brad.

When the bell rang, Candice left the class with a heavy heart.

"Candice."

Even the sound of his voice put her on edge. Candice adjusted the strap of her backpack and walked faster.

"Leave me alone, Brad." She didn't want to see him or speak to him. How could he throw his betrayal in her face after everything they'd been through?

Brad laid a surprisingly gentle hand on her arm to stop her. Willow was nowhere in sight.

"Have you decided?" he asked.

Of course. He was asking if she'd made a decision about the baby.

"Do you care?" she spat, whirling around to face him.

Brad stiffened; his hand dropped away and clenched into a fist. "Of course, I care! I don't want anything to happen to you. I know I messed up, but I never lied to you about how I felt." Brad ran a hand through his tousled hair. "Look, I spoke to a lady at an abortion clinic across town. It will be quick, painless, and then both of our lives can go on. No regrets, no problems. We messed up. Let me fix this for us."

He sounded so sincere, and Candice remembered a time before when he was her world.

"Here. Tell me you'll think about it." He handed her a small, white card, bearing the name and details of Meadowvale Planned Parenthood Clinic.

The dread that sat like a rock in Candice's stomach grew into a boulder. Still, she reached out a hesitant hand and swiped the card from Brad.

"I'll think about it." Candice had already been thinking about it. So, why was her decision wavering now that in the palm of her hand, she was holding the card that could solve all her problems?

Brad smiled. It was a small smile, filled with sadness and regret. Candice walked away from him, continuing down the hall until she found Jack waiting for her outside their math class.

"I saw you with Brad just now. Are you okay?" Jack asked. Tender concern glowed from him. Not a hint of jealousy shone in his eyes. Why did she expect there to be?

"I'm fine," Candice rubbed her hands anxiously. "It was just some unfinished business."

"Anything I can help with?"

"No, but I would love a hug." It was the most forward Candice had ever been with Jack, but she desperately needed the comfort.

With a happy sigh, Jack pulled her into his arms. The warmth of his strong embrace surrounded her, warming something in her that she hadn't known was cold. By the time he freed her, she had enough control of her emotions to smile without effort.

Anger gnawed at Jack as he watched Brad and Willow kiss on their way into the dark gym. He held Candice tighter, not wanting her to face Brad's betrayal. Despite what she had said, he knew the sight would hurt her.

Heart hammering behind his breastbone, he held Candice close to him. Her soft frame melted into his. She felt right. *They* felt right. But what now? Someone cleared their throat, and Candice and Jack jumped apart. They turned to see Mr. Phillips, a pile of test papers in his hand, waiting for them to take their seats in the classroom. Flushed, they quickly sat.

"Sorry," Candice mouthed to Jack.

Jack smiled and shook his head. There was nothing to forgive. He glanced at Candice once again, marveling at her beauty.

Focus, Anson.

Mr. Phillips walked around the classroom and handed out the test papers. Jack concentrated on his test and let his thoughts of Candice fall to the wayside as he began to write. When the last question was answered, Jack looked over at Candice again. Her auburn hair fell like a thick curtain as she bent over the desk, and her delicate fingers curled around her pencil as she scribbled across her page. Tender emotion pushed into his chest so strong, he laid his hand on his thumping heart. He'd never felt like this about a girl before, and the intensity scared him.

"Is everyone done?" Mr. Phillips walked around the class, collecting papers.

A murmur of "yes, sir" circled the room just before the bell rang, signaling the end of the lesson.

"How do you think you did?" Jack asked Candice as she packed her bag.

"Okay, I think. Number six was tricky—I couldn't remember if we'd studied that section or not." They walked into the hallway and leaned against a wall. Jack used his body to shield her from the flowing traffic.

"We did. Don't worry. I'm sure you did great!"

Candice scrunched her nose. "So, will you keep tutoring me?"

"Of course. I don't know how you made it this far without me."

It seemed natural for him to reach out and squeeze her hand, and to his pleasant surprise, she held on when he tried to let go.

"It's okay," she said softly. A pretty pink flush filled her cheeks, and a shy smile lifted her lips.

"You sure?" he asked, feeling a matching blush across his cheeks.

"Yes."

Drawn to her, he stepped closer, and he quickly found himself falling headfirst into her warm, brown eyes. Rational thought left Jack, and there was only want. He wanted to kiss her. His hand cupped her cheek and tilted her face up to his. Warring with himself, he blinked and dropped his hand, breaking their connection. Candice's warm, brown eyes gazed at him in wonder.

"I'll see you after school." Her lips bent in a small smile as she side-stepped him and walked briskly to her next class. Jack slung his backpack over his shoulder and whistled as he walked, his heart thrumming in his chest.

CHAPTER TWELVE

How could something so small feel like it weighed the same as a ton of bricks?

Black printed words on a white background, a small, green emblem stamped on top. The card rattled as it shook. Black numbers blended together in front of her crisscrossing eyes.

Was this really the right thing to do? Unconsciously, Candice ran her hand over her flat stomach. There was another living being inside of her. The idea still felt so foreign.

Her lips pressed together, and she clicked her tongue. A flick of her wrist sent the card flying onto her bed. She needed to think. Her stomach growled. Cancel that. She needed food and possibly a lobotomy.

In the kitchen, Mrs. Potter was preparing supper—chicken parmesan, Candice guessed, by the delightful smell in the room.

"Hi, Candice. How was school today?" she asked.

"It was fine." No need to mention her run-in with Brad. "I had a math test today."

"And?"

"It went really well, thanks to Jack."

Mrs. Potter paused her stirring and looked at Candice an eyebrow raised. "Is that the young man that took you to school this morning?"

Candice nodded and sat down on a black bar stool beside the marble island. She took an orange from the fruit basket and began to peel the skin off the fruit.

"Does he know about the baby?"

"No." Mrs. Potter frowned, and Candice felt her disappointment. "I did speak to Brad, though."

Mrs. Potter's frown deepened. "And what did he have to say?"

"He gave me the number of the abortion clinic across town. He wants me to end the pregnancy."

Mrs. Potter's frown turned in a scowl. "How do you feel about that?"

"I don't know." The rock in her stomach got heavier. "It makes the most sense. If I do it, then there's nothing to tell Jack; I don't disappoint my dad; and my mom . . . well, who knows what she'd think."

"My girl, I would hope after all of these years that you would take my opinion into consideration, too." Mrs. Potter sounded hurt.

Guilt pressed into her. "I know what you want me to do, Mrs. Potter, but it makes no sense. If I keep the . . . the baby, I might as well give up my life."

Mrs. Potter took the sauce off the stove and put a lid on it to keep it warm. She untied her apron and sat down beside Candice. Soft, familiar hands curled around Candice's. Love and understanding flowed from those hands.

"In Psalm 139:13-16, it says, 'For you created my inmost being; you knit me together in my mother's womb. I praise you because I am fearfully and wonderfully made . . . My frame was not hidden from you when I was made in the secret place, when I was woven together in the depths of the earth. Your eyes saw my unformed body; all the days ordained for me were written in your book before one of them came to be.'

"Candice, being pregnant is not a *mistake*. God knew before you were even born this would happen, even though it seems unexpected and scary to you. I know this is not what you planned, but God has a plan and purpose for your baby, no matter how he or she came into being."

"But this baby has cost me so much already! Brad left me for Willow, and now my friends won't even speak to me. And I'm sure that if Jack finds out, he'll be gone, too. It's too much, and I don't want it. I don't want this!" Candice pushed her chair back and ran up the stairs, ignoring Mrs. Potter's pleas for her to return to the kitchen.

This was all too much. The baby—*it*—was too much.

Tears streamed down her face as she picked up the white card and dialed the number listed.

"Meadowvale Planned Parenthood. How can I help you?" a kind, elderly lady answered.

"My name is Candice. I would like to make an appointment to see a doctor as soon as possible."

"For what, dear?"

The words stuck in her throat, but she forced them out. "I'm seventeen, and . . . I'm pregnant."

"Would tomorrow work for you?" the lady asked, quickly understanding her unspoken request. How many girls has she had the same conversation with?

Sickness and guilt crept up into Candice's throat, and her stomach revolted. "Tomorrow's fine. Thank you." The words gushed out like a tidal wave, only emptiness left in their path.

"All right, Candice. I'll just need a bit more information from you."

A few minutes later, the appointment was made, and her fate was sealed. Candice lay back against her bedcover and tried her best not to think. She was doing the right thing—not just for her, but for everyone. Her stomach churned; her heart raced; and although she was starving, she didn't think she could eat.

Hunger drove her downstairs later that evening. Mrs. Potter met her at the bottom of the stairs.

"Candice," Mrs. Potter began.

"I made an appointment at the clinic tomorrow," Candice cut her off. The words felt like hot acid as they slipped over her tongue.

Anguish broke Mrs. Potter's composure. "I didn't raise you like this, Candice. I didn't raise you to be a coward!" Her words were soft, but the gravity of them sat like the weight of a mountain on Candice's chest, so heavy, they could suffocate her.

"Candice, you know I love you." Mrs. Potter released a loud sigh. "God is still with you. He loves you. He loves and created the child you carry. Please don't do this."

"I'm sorry." Her resolve wavered, but then she imagined the faces of her father and Jack should they find out about the pregnancy. She couldn't disappoint them. "I don't have another choice."

"Of course, you do. Candice, there is always a choice. I pray you change your mind."

"I'm sorry. I can't."

Candice turned on her heel and ran back up the stairs, her hunger chased away by Mrs. Potter's despair and disappointment. Sobs shook her body as she lay on crumpled sheets. Tomorrow, it would all be over. Tomorrow, she would get her life back.

When tomorrow finally came, Candice avoided Jack. She just had to make it through school, and then she would be free. She sought solace in the library again, and when Jack tried to find her within the aisles, she sank into their shadows and hoped they would hide her from him. The day blurred on. Her phone pinged and rang a few times, but she ignored it, too. When the last bell of the day finally rang, Candice raced to her car, oblivious to the voices that called to her. She didn't want to see anyone; she didn't want to speak to anyone.

She closed the car door with a slam and twisted her key in the ignition. The engine roared to life humming over the rushing in her ears.

"Candice?"

I'm sorry, Jack, she thought as she shifted her car into gear and sped out of the lot. A quick glance in her rear-view mirror revealed Jack on the sidewalk, brow furrowed. Her heart squeezed. Tomorrow, it would be okay.

As she drove to Meadowvale Clinic, Candice choked down the last of her crackers and ginger beer and braced her heart against the emotions she didn't want to feel. A lump formed in her throat, and she fought to swallow it back.

I'm doing the right thing. Right?

She turned the last corner and brought her car to a halt. Taking a deep breath, she stared at the white building that was so deceptive in its innocence. Again, her mind warred with itself. Was she doing the right thing?

There is always a choice.

Mrs. Potter's words circled her mind. What was she doing here? It seemed like the best choice—the only choice she had. She dropped her head onto the steering wheel, the world going dark behind her closed eyes. She imagined her father's gentle smile turning into sharp disappointment as she told him, followed by Brad's sneer, and then Jack's. The tender expression Jack always wore changed into disgust as he looked at her. No, there wasn't another choice, at least not for her.

"Honey? Honey, are you all right?" a concerned voice asked. Candice jumped in her seat and whipped her head around to see a woman outside her door.

Lily Anson. Jack's mom.

A low groan escaped her. Could this get any worse? Heart beating furiously, Candice tried to gather her thoughts and rolled down her car window.

"Candice? Is that you?"

"Hi, Mrs. Anson." Her voice came out softer than a whisper, shame taking hold.

"You can call me Lily, remember? What are you doing here?" Her eyes were gentle.

Candice was trapped. She couldn't lie. There was no other explanation.

"I . . . I made an appointment here."

Lily's eyes filled with warm concern. She nodded in understanding. "I see. Why don't we sit a while, and you can tell me all about it?"

Feeling like years had passed since she'd left school, Candice got out of her car. She lifted the trunk door and sat. Lily sat beside her.

"Pregnant?"

Candice nodded.

"How many weeks?"

"Ten, I think."

Lily hummed in thought. "You know, I don't usually come to places like this. I try and speak to girls before it reaches this point;

but for some reason, I felt the need to come by today." She smiled at Candice. "God told me to come here."

Was this an answer to Mrs. Potter's prayer? Had God sent Lily to help Candice? Did God actually care?

"Jack didn't do this." Candice said gesturing down to her stomach. "The . . . the baby's father and I broke up. Jack has been a great friend to me through it all. Well, as close of a friend as I'll allow right now."

Lily moved closer, her expression soft and gentle. "He's been in knots all day. I spoke to him on the drive over."

Anxiety twisted her insides. "I was too ashamed to tell him. It was one time. Just *one* time. I didn't know it could happen so quickly. Brad and I broke up, and then Jack happened . . . "

Empathy poured from Lily. "Most girls your age don't expect it to happen to them. I'm sorry this happened to you, Candice, but I'm not sorry I came here today. Your baby deserves a chance at life. They are not a mistake."

Candice shifted; her mind raced. Mrs. Potters' words played over and over again like a broken record. *Her choice. A gift of God. Not an accident.*

"Is this really what you want, Candice?" Lily gestured to the abortion clinic. "This road won't be as easy as they lead you to believe."

Candice's hand trembled as she laid it on her stomach. A baby. There was a baby inside of her.

"No . . . no, I don't want to kill it—kill the baby. My baby." It was a strange emotion that calmed her heart. "But I don't think I'm strong enough to handle it alone."

"But you're not alone," Lily said. "Why don't you come with me to the Save a Life Center, and we can talk about this more?"

The dark cloud of despair Candice had carried all day lifted off her shoulders, and a ray of light began to peek through. It was as if a small voice was telling her that if she went with Lily, everything would be okay.

Candice nodded. "I'll follow you there."

Lily smiled and stood. She walked back to her car and waited at the exit for Candice to follow.

Feeling hopeful for the first time since she'd taken the pregnancy test, Candice started up her car and turned onto the road, leaving Meadowvale Clinic in the distance.

CHAPTER THIRTEEN

Jack shuffled back into the school and walked to his locker. The memory of the grim set of Candice's lips and the sad light in her eyes circled in his mind. Why was Candice avoiding him? Had he spooked her somehow? And where had she gone in such a hurry?

Candice, where are you? From the beginning, he'd made no secret of his interest in her. Maybe he'd come on too strong and scared her? *Or maybe she's not as over Brad as she told you she was.* The thought settled like a hard rock inside his stomach.

And then there were the rumors.

Frustrated, Jack scrubbed his hand through his hair and ripped open his locker door.

"Hey, man, are you okay?" Christian walked up beside him. His face was filled with concern for Jack.

"Yeah, it's just . . . Candice is avoiding me."

"Do you know why? Have you asked her about the rumors?" Christian asked. "Come on, Jack. Everyone has heard them."

"I was hoping she'd talk to me. Trust me enough to tell me. I mean, I really like her, man. She's kind and funny, and when she laughs . . . " Jack shook his head. "I'm such a fool."

Christian chuckled. "No, you're a good guy, and unfortunately, even the good guys get hurt."

Jack sighed and was about to agree when his phone rang, immediately stalling the breath in his chest. He swiped the phone open and brought it to his ear.

"Candice?" he asked immediately.

The voice on the other end wasn't the one he'd been hoping for.

"Hi, Jack. It's Mom," his mother answered sweetly.

"Oh. Sorry, Mom. It's been a rough day."

"You want to tell me about it?"

Jack and Christian started their trek out of the school building as he explained. "Candice was acting strange all day. First, she wouldn't talk to me; then she wouldn't answer any of my texts; and then she practically sped away from me in the parking lot! I'm losing my mind worrying about her."

"She's probably going through something and just needs a bit of time. I'm sure she'll talk to you when she's ready," his mom reassured.

She was probably right. Candice just needed some time. "Yeah, maybe. Are we still on to help you at the Save a Life Center this afternoon?"

"Yes—I have a quick stop to make, and then I'll meet you guys there," she said.

"Thanks, Mom. I love you."

"Love you, too. Bye!"

Jack slid the phone into his pocket and slung his backpack higher up on his shoulder.

"Your mom still needs us to help her move furniture at the clinic?" Christian asked, glancing down at his phone to check the time.

"Yeah, let's get going."

Jack climbed into his truck and trailed Christian to the center.

What if the rumors were true? What if Candice *was* actually pregnant? Is that what Brad had meant when he'd asked Jack to look after her?

An old Buddy Holly song crooned on the radio, and he turned the volume up, hoping to drown out his busy thoughts. It was useless, though. All he could think about was Candice and how she was pushing him away. He slammed the gear shift into park and hoped out of the car. Maybe some hard work would help take his mind off Candice.

"What time did your mom say again?" Christian leaned against the hood of his car and checked his phone.

"Four-thirty." Jack checked his watch. Four-forty-five. Where was his mother?

The red sedan Jack knew belonged to his mother's friend and colleague, Veronica, was parked just outside the glass doors of the Center. His mother's blue SUV was nowhere to be found.

"Mom said to meet her here. She said she was on her way somewhere but would be back as soon as possible."

"Anyway, you want to tell me what you're going to do if that rumor turns out to be true?"

"I don't know, man." Truthfully, Jack didn't want to think about the possibility of Candice being pregnant. In fact, he'd made a point of *not* thinking about it.

"I know you like her, but . . . " Christian trailed off.

He didn't need to finish his thought; Jack knew what he was going to say. Could he overlook the fact that Candice had been with Brad? An uneasy confusion pulled at Jack. What would he do if Candice were pregnant? Ignore her like her friends were doing at school? Stay away from her and pretend that she didn't make his heart race faster or he didn't miss her when she wasn't around? And then there was the promise he'd made to Brad to take care of her. A part of him welcomed the idea of taking care of her. But what if there was a baby that came with the package? What would he do then?

God, what do I do? Please show me.

His mother's car turned into the parking lot, followed closely by Candice's SUV. In startling clarity, Jack had his answer, and everything made sense. Candice climbed out of her car and glued herself to his mother's side. Her hands trembled as she twisted them together, unwilling to meet his gaze.

"Jack." She didn't seem surprised to see him. In fact, she looked relieved. Relieved to have her secret out?

"Candice," he said, voice soft with surprise.

"I guess you know why I'm here?"

"You're pregnant." It wasn't a question.

Candice hunched further into herself, and Jack reached out to touch her before stopping himself.

"Brad?" He didn't know why he asked. He already knew.

Candice nodded. She looked so small and scared that his protective instinct roared back to life. Instead of the anger he expected, there was only blinding jealousy and pain. Not *at* Candice, but *for* her. How could Brad have left her in this alone?

She looked up at him, pleading in the depth of her eyes, and his other emotions swept away, leaving him drowning in a pool of confusion once again.

"I'm glad you boys could come today," Lily said. "Jack, why don't you and Christian meet me in Veronica's office? Candice, you can come with me." She took Candice's hand and led her away. Jack stopped himself from following, unsure what he should even say to her.

After a moment, Christian tapped Jack on the shoulder, and he mechanically followed him through the glass doors. Candice had already made her way down the hall and into one of the private rooms, but Lily hung back, waiting to give Jack and Christian more details about what she needed help with.

"Can you two start by moving the blue sofas in Veronica's office into the main lounge? It's a bit later than I'd like, so if you don't mind hurrying, I'd appreciate it. I need you to be out of here before the afternoon session lets out," Lily said.

"Sure, Mrs. A. Jack and I will be done as soon as we can. Come on, Jack."

Lily ducked into what Jack assumed was Candice's room, and the boys left to get to work. Motion detection lights flickered on as Jack and Christian walked down the white hallway and stopped outside of a beautifully carved wooden door. It had a picture of a mountain stream and a flock of birds. Jack had lost count of the number of times he'd seen it, but today, for some reason, it made him think of freedom.

"Jack, are you with me?" Christian asked as he opened the door.

"What? Yeah," Jack mumbled.

"So . . . It's true then."

"I guess. I'd hoped it wasn't. That it was just another rumor running around the school. Man, she's pregnant. What am I going to do?"

"I don't know, but I'm here for you whatever you decide," Christian said firmly.

God, what do I do? Desperate, silent prayers bled from his heart as they maneuvered furniture from one room to the next. His thoughts stayed on Candice. How was she? What was she discussing with his mother?

As if she'd heard his thoughts, his mom popped her head into the room.

"Are you boys done yet?" she asked.

"Almost, Mom. Is there anything else you need us to do?" He was tired and confused, and he really wanted to find Candice.

"No, I think that's all. Thank you," she said. Then with gentle and knowing eyes, she said the words Jack had been hoping for. "Would you like to see Candice before you leave?"

Jack nodded anxiously, and the two boys followed her down the hall and into Candice's room. Once they were inside, Jack's eyes roved over her face. Her normally pink cheeks were pale, and her brown eyes were puffy and rimmed in red. She'd been crying. As he looked, one thing become noticeably clear to him: he cared about her. Much more than he had been willing to admit to himself. Ignoring his mom and Christian, Jack surrendered to the pull he felt toward her. Arms that ached to hold and comfort her wrapped around her waist, and to his delight, Candice melted against him.

"I'm not going anywhere." He whispered the words meant for her and her alone. Her soft cheek felt like silk as he kissed it. Tenderly, he let her go and smiled. "I'll see you later."

Nodding to Christian, Jack headed out, smiling at the pride he saw flowing from his mother's eyes.

Lily chuckled as Jack and Christian left. "Although I would want the situation different, don't assume that Jack doesn't want you like this. Jack knows more than most boys his age and is more mature than them. He's also loving, charming, and the most giving man I know. And I'm not just saying that because I'm his mother—I really mean it."

Candice already knew all those things about Jack. But would he be different from Brad when it really mattered?

I'm not going anywhere.

Lily grinned. "Why don't you follow me, Candice? I'd like for you to meet someone."

She led Candice out of the small waiting room to meet a woman a few years older than Lily. The woman's flowing white hair was set in a messy bun on the top of her head, and a kind smile matched the glow in her deep green eyes.

"Hiya, Candice. I'm Veronica. Lily tells me you're expecting a baby." Veronica reminded her of Mrs. Potter—happiness bottled in a person.

"Y-yes." Had the last few minutes actually happened? Was it her imagination? *Face it, Candice, even your imagination isn't that good.*

"Well, come on in. Let's see that gorgeous baby of yours." Veronica welcomed Candice into a larger room. Soft pastel paint covered the walls, and a large beige shag rug lay under two cream-colored chairs. In one corner of the room, there was a bed that looked like it belonged in hospital and a white machine with lots of buttons and things that looked like wands.

Veronica walked over to the bed and patted it. "Make yourself comfortable. We're going to do a sonar scan of the baby. That way, we can tell how far along you are and whether the baby is growing at a normal rate or not."

"O-okay," Candice said. Cold but soft cushions pressed into her as she leaned into the mattress and rested against the raised head.

Lily rubbed her shoulder. "Overwhelmed?"

"Yes." Candice felt her hands tingle.

"Don't be scared. This won't hurt you or the baby," Lily said. "It will just be a bit cold on your stomach."

Calmed by Lily's gentle reassurance, Candice relaxed and let Veronica lift her shirt up slightly to get access to her stomach. Veronica took a wand from the machine and put some sort of thick gel on the device. Candice shivered as the cool gel made contact with her stomach. A few seconds later, the sound of a steady *thump thump* filled the room.

"What's that?" Candice asked.

"The most beautiful sound in the world—the sound of a healthy baby's heartbeat." Veronica's smile widened. "Here, have a look."

Veronica turned a small screen to face Candice. In black and white, the image of a small, perfect baby kicked and stretched in its home. An all-encompassing love filled Candice.

"That's my baby?" Candice breathed the words, tears streaming down her cheeks. A baby. *Her* baby. There was a small life inside of her belly.

Veronica typed on the keyboard a few times; it looked like she was drawing lines and taking measurements. "Yes, that cute little grape-sized baby is yours. You're about ten weeks?"

A smile that came from deep inside Candice blossomed on her face. "That sounds about right."

CHAPTER FOURTEEN

Fear replaced the wonder Candice had been feeling just a few minutes ago. There was a baby inside her—a small life, totally dependent on her. A cold sweat formed on her brow, her breath sawing in and out of her lungs. Veronica wiped the gel from her stomach and left the room.

"Candice?" Lily wrapped her arm around Candice's shoulders and helped her sit up on the narrow bed. Lily then guided her to one of the chairs on the other side of the room.

"Just breathe. It's okay. Just breathe. You're not alone. We've got you." Lily gently guided Candice's head down to rest between her knees. Air rushed in and out of Candice's lungs. She focused on Lily's quiet voice murmuring comforting words. The tightness in her chest slowly relaxed with each word Lily spoke. "It's okay, Candice. It's okay. We've got you."

After what seemed like an eternity, Candice's lungs drew deep breaths, and her heart rate calmed. The soft, circular motions of Lily's hand brought her back.

"I think I'm okay now." She rested against the chair's wide back and breathed slowly. Lily's arm eased from her shoulder and moved to hold her hand.

"I'm just glad you didn't pass out." This obviously wasn't the first time Lily had dealt with a neurotic teenager.

"Me, too. I'm sorry."

"Don't be. Most girls typically do one of two things when they realize what they've really gotten themselves into—pass out or cry. I'm usually ready for both." Lily shrugged and fished out a pack of tissues from her pocket.

A faint giggle escaped Candice. "So, not your first rodeo?"

"No, not by a long shot. This is what we do here at the Save a Life Center. Every day, we have girls like you come through our doors, desperate for love, acceptance, and yes, even answers and a place to stay. You'd be surprised how some parents behave when their child has disappointed them. Have you told your parents?"

"No. My mom is never around, and my dad . . . well, this would kill him." Horrible guilt chewed at Candice. Her father deserved to know.

"And that's why you went to Meadowvale Clinic?"

"Yes. I didn't know what else to do."

"Candice, I'm not going to lie to you and tell you that it's going to be easy if you decide to keep your baby. It's not. You'll have to deal with prejudice, snarky comments, disappointment, and disapproval. But I can promise you something: if you choose to keep your baby and either raise it yourself or place the baby for adoption, it will bring you better peace than the alternative."

Lily didn't have to say the word "abortion." After all, that was the only alternative there really was, and now that Candice had seen that little life, there was no way she could willingly end it.

"Do you believe in God?" Lily asked gently.

"I . . . don't know. Maybe? Mrs. Potter, my nanny, talks about God often. She's kind of like my mom, and she told me God loves me and the baby, despite how my baby was conceived. She also said God has a good plan for me and my baby."

"It sounds like your nanny is a wise woman. And she is absolutely right. God loves you and your baby so much, Candice. He wants only what's best for you; that is why we are told in the Bible that lovemaking should only be between a man and woman who are married. Not just because of the intimacy such an act includes, but also because of the natural outcome of such an act. God didn't mean for moms or dads to raise their babies alone. He meant for them to be raised within a loving relationship between the baby's parents," Lily explained gently. "That being said, it doesn't mean that God loves you less because your baby was conceived this way. He wants to be with you, if you'll let Him come into your life. You can't do this alone, Candice. You aren't strong enough alone, but with God, you can do the impossible."

Deep in her heart, something beckoned her. It was that still, small Voice, asking to come in and be with her. To come in and help.

"God loves you so much. He wants to be your Strength and Guiding Light; there is forgiveness in Him, not only for yourself but also for the anger you feel toward Brad and what he took from you. Let God into your life. Let Him carry you."

The tugging in her heart increased, and Candice felt tears brewing behind her eyes. Lily looked at the glistening in her eyes and knew Candice's soul was at the precipice of something great.

"May I pray with you?" Lily asked.

A lump stuck in Candice's throat. She nodded.

Lily bowed her head and put her hands on Candice's shoulders. Candice bowed her head and let Lily's words flow over her, echoing her words in her heart.

"Dear Heavenly Father, please come into my life." Lily prayed the words for Candice. "Please help me to make the right decision concerning this baby. I want to do what is right. Give me the strength I need. In Jesus' Name. Amen."

When Candice opened her eyes, the same peace and understanding she felt was reflected in Lily's eyes. Her expression was peaceful—a peace that Candice felt and cherished.

"Candice." Lily spoke softly but with conviction. "I urge you to carry your baby to term. I can put you in touch with a Christian adoption agency, where I am sure a good home with loving parents could be found for your baby. Your baby deserves a chance at life. God will not love you less, no matter what you decide, but the alternative comes with a heavy price. It's a price that I wouldn't want you or any other girl I've worked with to pay. The thought of 'what if' or 'what might have been' will haunt you for the rest of your life."

Her choice was made, and only peace flowed from it.

"I've made my decision. I'm going to have my baby," Candice said. Resolve settled the storm inside her, and her hope grew. She wasn't alone anymore, and it was all going to be okay.

Lily smiled wide, her eyes reflecting Candice's joy. "I'm *so* glad, Candice. There is a long road ahead, but I know you can do it."

For the next hour, Lily answered all Candice's questions about pregnancy, adoption, and anything else she wanted. Mrs. Potter was right again, and Candice could feel the thankfulness deep in her bones.

"One more thing before you go: there is a teenage pregnancy support group that meets here in the afternoons. I can give you the details if you would like to attend. Here's my number. Call me whenever you need," Lily said.

"Thank you, Lily. I appreciate all you've done for me," Candice said, overwhelmed by Lily's kindness.

"You're welcome. Be gentle on yourself; the next few months will be tough enough."

Candice waved goodbye to Lily and walked out of the building feeling like a new person. Whole and changed. She climbed into her car and drove off, eager to speak to Jack and Mrs. Potter.

There was a car in the driveway when she returned home; however, it was not the car she had expected or hoped for. What was her mother doing here? Something had to be wrong. The porch light flickered on as Candice approached. Just before she reached the wooden porch, her mother came hustling out of the house, a laptop in one hand and an overnight bag in the other. Another unplanned trip.

Mentally shoring up her courage, Candice prepared to tell her mother about the baby. It was probably now or never.

"Hi, Mom. Do you have a minute?"

Her mother paused her trek to her car, her hand resting on the trunk of her black Mercedes.

"Candice? When did you get here?" her mother asked.

"A couple of seconds ago. Are you going away again?"

"Yes, my client in Chicago is having a meltdown over a book signing in a few hours. If I leave now, I'll get there right before he has to show up."

Candice nodded, steadying her resolve.

"Okay, well, I guess I better hurry then." Tell her. Another opportunity probably wouldn't come for a while. She took a deep breath. "Mom, I'm . . . I'm pregnant, and I've decided to have the baby."

The fictitious smile that usually hovered on her mother's gloss-covered lips froze. Then, her eye went wide, and her expression settled into something firm and unhappy.

"Is this some kind of joke to get my attention, Candice?" A disapproving frown bent her mother's lovely features.

"What? No, Mom." Hurt and anger rose in equal measure. She should have known. "You know what, just forget it. Have a safe trip." Candice brushed past her mother and let herself into the house, barely suppressing her disappointment. A firm hand grabbed her arm.

"You're serious?" The front door closed with a decisive bang behind her mother.

"Yes. I'm about ten weeks along, and I'm going to place the baby for adoption."

"Candice, I . . . uh, I don't know what to say. If this meeting weren't so important, I would cancel. But I should be back in a few days, and then we can discuss this, okay?" her mother said.

Had Candice really expected this to go any differently? Maybe. Anyway, there was nothing she could do about it now.

"Have a safe trip, Mom," she said. She gave her mom a quick hug and watched her hurry out the door, her black car leaving again like Candice had seen so many times before.

Candice swiped open her phone; she really needed to speak to Jack. The phone rang and rang until, finally, she heard his voice—unfortunately, it was his voicemail.

Uneasiness pushed against her newfound joy. Candice felt her mind start to spin in circles again, only this time, she wasn't wondering about herself. She was wondering about Jack and if he was avoiding her.

CHAPTER FIFTEEN

Jack changed his mind for the dozenth time. He was so sure he could be there for Candice when he'd seen her at the Center. But now as he watched the peewee league run up and down the basketball court, the pregnant mothers gathered like a gaggle of geese next to the court, laughing and sharing stories, he wasn't so sure. Surely, it should be simple: boy likes girl; boy asks girl out; they fall in love and live happily ever after. Simple. But what happens when the girl has a baby with another man? What then?

Jack shook his head. This wasn't helping anything. After practice, Jack returned home and flopped onto his bed, tired and confused. His phone buzzed in his pocket.

Candice.

He watched the screen as the phone rang, wrestling with himself until it went black. What was he going to do? There was only One Who knew. Jack slid off the side of his bed, his knees balanced on the wooden floor as he lay his head between his hands.

Lord, please . . .

It wasn't until after the sun disappeared below the horizon that Jack finally stood, stretching out his stiff knees. He reached for his phone and dialed Candice's number. Now, he was sure.

"Hello?"

"Candice, it's Jack."

"Jack. Oh, Jack, I'm so sorry. I should have told you sooner. I'm so sorry." Candice voice rose with the level of her hysteria as she tried to explain.

"Shh, it's all right. Can we talk?" He tried to clear the emotion from his throat, hurting for her desperation.

"Sure. Do you want me to meet you somewhere?" Candice's voice wobbled with anxiety.

"How about I just come to your house? Is that okay?"

"Okay." Her voice went soft, as if accepting something inevitable as she hung up.

Jack stared at the blank phone screen, dread growing in his stomach. Had she misunderstood him? Taking the steps two at a time, Jack ran out the house to his car, praying that Candice hadn't heard him wrong.

It couldn't be healthy the way her heart raced in her chest. Jack was coming over to tell her goodbye. She was sure of it. Preparing herself for the worst, Candice sipped on a cup of tea, the calming chamomile and sweet peppermint warming her frigid veins. Mrs. Potter had gone home for the day, but she would come back to check on Candice just before bedtime. She startled at the loud bang of an old truck door being closed in the quiet of the night.

This is it.

Candice wrapped her arms around her middle and held tight, hoping against hope that she was wrong. She watched Jack through the large bay window. Would this be the last time she saw him? He paused in the bright light of the full moon and took a deep breath, muttering to himself. An agitated hand rushed through his hair, and then he took the last steps toward the door.

Ding dong. The old doorbell pealed, and even though she knew it was coming, she still jumped at the sound.

Breathe, Candice. You might be wrong.

She swung the door open, and her hope melted faster than snow on a sunny day when she saw the dark look on Jack's face.

She stiffened her spine. She wouldn't cry. Not again.

"Look, Jack, I know why you came. It's okay. Me and my baby aren't your problem. I would never ask that of you. You've been a great friend. Thank you. I guess this is goodbye, then?"

The words rushed over themselves as they spilled out from between her trembling lips. With the last of her courage, she tried to close the door on him, unwilling to look him in the face. The door wouldn't move. She tried again. It was just as unyielding as the first time she'd tried.

Finally, she looked up. Jack still waited at the door, arm extended and hand planted firmly against its surface. The overwhelming acceptance and firm resolve in his eyes left her weak with relief and fear-filled hope. Her hand fell from the door as he swung it open all the way and collected her into his arms.

His lips landed on hers, first urgent and then gentle. Loving and accepting and steady. The clocked ticked over once, twice, thrice before he pulled away from her mouth and gathered her close.

"I meant what I said earlier. I'm not going anywhere. I want to be with you, baby and all." Jack kissed her again and then pressed her head to his chest. She could hear the rapid thumping of his heart. "Now, do you still want to be with me?"

The vulnerability in his voice cut her to the core. She stared in wonderment at the boy in front of her, his cheeks flushed and his eyes alight with fondness for her. He waited expectantly, shifting nervously as the moments ticked by.

"Uh, any minute now." He shifted his feet. "Sorry, I know this is a lot to process." He released her and stepped back running his hand along the back of his neck.

"Oh!" Hope expanded like a balloon inside her. "Oh, Jack. So much! I mean, yes, I still want you if you still want me."

Jack slowly smiled. "Always." His warm hand closed over hers, and he tugged her close again. "Do you want to get out of here? Maybe grab a bite to eat?"

"Yes, please, I'm starving. Let me get some water and my coat." Candice flew up the stairs and danced around her room, squealing like a mad squirrel before she rushed back to Jack. Joy overflowed in her. The next months would be tough, but with God and Jack standing by her and her baby, it would be all right.

"Okay, I'm ready." As she entered the room, Jack's gorgeous smile greeted her. Dumbstruck again, she stared at him.

After a long moment, warm color filled Jack's cheeks. "Candice?" he asked.

"Sorry," she said. "I missed that smile almost as much I missed you today."

Chuckling, Jack walked closer, brushing his lips on hers. "Come on, Miss Smile. Let's get you something to eat."

"That sounds heavenly."

Taking her hand again, Jack pulled her out of the house and to his waiting car.

Music from the country radio station filled Jack's car as he drove. "How did your talk with my mom at the Center go?" he asked.

"It went really well. I'm going to carry the baby to term, and then I think I want to place him or her for adoption. I'm not ready to be a mom. I know now it's the right decision for me and for my baby. I know the next six months are going to be hard, but I also know that God loves me and my baby." Candice smiled and nudged Jack. "Your mom helped me realize that. And now that I know, I could never abort my baby."

Jack reached over and entwined their fingers. "I can live with that. God and I had a long discussion, and I decided I want to be with you, baby and all. I know things are going to be tough, and we're probably up against a lot, but I believe we can make it. Are you with me in this?"

Candice smiled warmly. "I feel the same. Are you really sure this is what you want?"

"With everything in me," he whispered. He brushed his lips over the back of her hand and laid their hands on his leg as he parked the car. To Candice's surprise, they were at the park, very near to the place they'd met not so long ago.

"What are we doing here? Aren't we getting something to eat?" Candice asked.

"Patience, Miss Pregnant," Jack teased. He helped her out of the car, kissing her thoroughly before leading her to a bustling food truck stationed nearby.

"Is pizza okay?" he said.

"Yep. Pepperoni sounds like angel food right now."

Chuckling again, Jack placed and paid for their order. A few minutes later, they sat on a wooden bench overlooking the lake and ate.

Candice wiped her mouth with her napkin, aware of the caring eyes watching her. "Do I have something on my face?"

Jack shook his head. "I missed you today," he said.

"I missed you, too. I was sure tonight would end up differently. I'm really grateful that it didn't."

Jack pushed his plate aside and placed an arm around her, tapping a gentle beat on her shoulder. "I spoke with Brad yesterday," he said. Candice's heart beat a little faster. Jack stared off into the distance in a world of his own. "He asked me to look after you." The way he said the words made her think of a solemn oath.

Candice stiffened.

"Hey, I didn't say that to upset you," Jack said. "I think he knows he made a terrible mistake." His other arm came around her to cuddle her closer, and he kissed her on the forehead. "You're really special to me, Candice."

"You're special to me, too." Candice toyed with her empty plate, thinking. "Jack? I want to introduce you to someone."

"Oh? Who?" he said curiously.

"Mrs. Potter."

His answering smile warmed her to the core. "I'd be happy to meet her."

They chatted about the day as they drove back to Candice's house. If happiness were a tangible thing, she'd just been handed it in a full basket. The house stood like a majestic sentinel in the sable sky. The security lamps burned like bright candles. A light shone from the kitchen.

"Mrs. Potter's already here. She's probably wondering where I am." They climbed out of the car and walked into the house.

"Candice, is that you?" Mrs. Potter called from somewhere in the house.

"Yes, and I brought someone I'd like you to meet." She tugged Jack by the hand in the direction of the kitchen.

He followed behind her, holding tightly as if he were afraid to let go. Smiling again, Candice turned into the kitchen.

"There you are, dear. Where have you been?" Candice ran up to Mrs. Potter, engulfing her in a hug. "Mrs. Potter there's so much to tell you, but first . . . " Candice gestured to Jack, drawing Mrs. Potter's attention. "Jack, this is Mrs. Potter. Mrs. Potter, this is Jack. He's my, uh . . . "

"I'm her boyfriend," Jack cut in. "If she'll have me, of course . . . " Jack shrugged and rubbed the back of his neck.

"Definitely," Candice said confidently.

"Well then, you come with me, and I'll decide if you're good enough for my Candice. Not like that other boy she was dating." Mrs. Potter thrust her hands into her ample hips and stared at Jack, eyes narrowed in suspicion.

Candice giggled at the alarmed expression on Jack's face. "Don't worry, she's harmless."

A solemnness descended over Jack's laughing blue eyes. "I assure you, I'm nothing like the other guy."

Candice shook her head, a tender smile on her face as she watched Jack and Mrs. Potter walk into a nearby room to continue their conversation. Then, there was a loud bang on the door, followed by the repeated ringing of the buzzer.

Startled, Candice walked warily to the door. Who on earth would come at this time of night? Her mother had a key.

Still, she opened the door and froze, stunned at who she saw standing there.

CHAPTER SIXTEEN

"Dad?" Candice let herself be engulfed into the warm, burly chest of her dad. Memories assaulted her as his familiar scent of cedarwood and fresh air filled her senses.

"Oh, my girl. You're okay," he muttered repeatedly. He squeezed her tighter and released a huge, pent-up breath.

"Are you okay?"

"I think the better question is are *you* okay? I got a frantic voicemail from Mrs. Potter this afternoon and raced over here as soon as I could. What is going on?"

The strain on her father's face broke Candice's heart. As much as she would have liked to tell him about the baby after he calmed down, her father's expression told her that there would be no waiting. She would have to tell him now.

"Why don't you sit in the living room? I'll get some tea and then we can talk," she said.

Her father must have heard the plea in her voice because he nodded. She gestured in the direction of the living room with her head.

"It's the room on the left. I'll be right back."

Candice watched him walk to the living room and sighed to herself. Tonight was turning out to be much more than she had bargained for.

Jack laughed at something Mrs. Potter said as Candice entered the kitchen.

"Who was at the door, dear?" Mrs. Potter asked, her expression entirely too innocent.

"Mrs. Potter, how could you?" Candice said, although the words were more exhausted than angry. She boiled the kettle and set a small tray with the makings for tea.

"You gave me no choice. I had a bad feeling this morning, and then when you raced out, I was sure you were on your way to . . . " Mrs. Potter trailed off, her eyes glistening. "You wouldn't listen to me. I had to do something."

Mrs. Potter suddenly looked old to Candice, her wrinkles emphasized by the concern lining her features. She'd stood by Candice's side for so many years and dealt with so much. Candice realized with an overwhelming rush of gratitude that she didn't want to take Mrs. Potter's presence for granted any more. She rushed forward and hugged Mrs. Potter close.

"I'm sorry. And you're right—I was on my way to have an abortion, but I'm keeping the baby. I'll tell you all about it after I've spoken to my dad."

"Your dad?" A deep frown bent Jack's brow. "Should I be worried?"

"Don't worry, tough guy. I'll tell him it wasn't you," she joked. Judging by the firm pinch of Jack's lips, it hadn't worked.

"Do you want me to come with you?" Always the protector—it was one of the many things she appreciated about him.

Candice smiled but shook her head.

"No, it's probably better that I talk to him alone. This could go two ways. I'm hoping for the better one."

With a filled teapot, sugar, and milk, Candice carried the tray of cups into the living room. She placed it on the wooden coffee table at the center of the room. Her dad was on his feet, his steps agitated.

Well, that's not a good sign.

"Come sit, Dad. Have your tea."

"Don't you—" He stopped himself and sighed. "All right." He sank into the sofa beside her, his weight rocking the tea in her cup. He took a few sips and placed the cup on the table.

"Okay, I've had the tea. Now, tell me what's going on."

Candice took a deep, steadying breath. Now that the moment was here, she didn't feel so brave.

"I'm pregnant." Her voice trembled with the effort of keeping it stable. She couldn't look at her dad. She didn't want to see the disappointment she was sure was on his face.

"What!"

Option two, then: the explosion.

"Who is he?" her father demanded. He was on his feet and pacing again. The furrow between his eyebrows had grown deeper with each passing second.

"It doesn't matter, Dad. He isn't in my life anymore." Candice reached for her father's arm and tried to tug him back to the sofa.

In that moment, Jack chose to walk into the room. He must've heard her father's roar and come to see if she was okay. Her father whirled on him and stuck an accusatory finger in Jack's direction.

"You? Is it you? Are you the one who's responsible for this? What have you done to my little girl?" he yelled.

Jack froze, stunned. He held his hands up in surrender. "Mr. Hillman, I think there's—"

"Get out! I don't want to see you around here again!" The vein in her dad's neck bulged under his skin, and his face was red with fury.

Candice stood in front of Jack with her arms outstretched. "No, Daddy. It's not him!" She pushed against his advancing form with all her might. She might have been a sapling pressing against a tractor for all the effect she had.

Jack was tall, but her dad was probably twice the size of him in width and hard muscle. And he was as angry as a bear. Jack glanced at her, his expression pleading.

"I'm okay," she mouthed to him.

He mouthed something back, but she couldn't understand. Jack had to leave, for his sake.

"Go," she pleaded.

Jack stopped, his mouth set in a hard line. "Candice . . ."

"Go, Jack," she said, firmly this time.

Muscles rigid, Jack turned then hurried out to his car. She didn't take her eyes off her father. She was so worried he would follow Jack and do something to him.

"He's not the one, Dad. It's not his baby!" Her voice rose louder, and she pushed her father back. At last, he relented, staring at the door Jack had left through. "He's the good guy," Candice crossed her arms over her chest and glared at her father.

Finally, her father returned his attention to Candice, but the damage was already done. Unable to face her father any longer, she spun on her heel and ran to her room. She threw herself onto her unmade bed and let the tears come.

Heart thundering, Jack's blood raced through his veins. Who did Candice's father think he was? Mr. Hillman hadn't even listened; he'd automatically assumed the worst. He smashed his hand into the steering wheel, frustration bubbling out.

Running up the steps of his porch, he slammed the door behind him so hard that it clattered in the frame.

"Jack? Is that you?" His mother walked into the entrance hall, a novel in one hand and a coffee mug in the other. "What happened? Is it Candice?"

Jack sagged against the door. "No, she's fine. We're fine. Her dad was there tonight. He didn't even let me speak, Mom."

"Follow me." His mom waved him into the kitchen. They sat opposite each other at the island. "Okay, start over. What happened?"

Jack filled his mother in on what had happened earlier in the evening. "And then while I was in the kitchen with Mrs. Potter, Candice's dad started shouting, so I went to see if she was okay. Then he starts shouting at me, saying, 'how could I do this to his daughter,' and even when Candice tried to reason with him, he wouldn't listen! Mom, he thinks I got Candice pregnant, and now he doesn't want me to see her again."

His mother drew a deep breath. "I'm sorry, Jack. I'm sure once he calms down, he will talk to Candice with a more rational mind and maybe reconsider his order. This must be a massive shock to him. Think about how you felt when you found out, and now think how Mr. Hillman must feel. The love and responsibility we feel for our children is hard to explain. Sometimes, we feel like we've failed when our children make a decision we don't agree with, whether it's good or bad. Candice made a choice, and her father probably feels like he's failed her in some way because if things were different and her parents hadn't divorced, she might not have made that decision to begin with. I know it's hard, Jack. Everyone's emotions are high right now. Let it cool down for the evening, and tomorrow we'll go and see them."

Jack reluctantly nodded. He'd been shocked when he'd found out, and the way his mom explained it made him realize it was likely ten times worse for Candice's father. It's a wonder he hadn't had a heart attack right then and there. "Thanks, Mom. What do you think about this whole thing?"

"Jack, I love you, and I want you to be happy. I know Candice makes you happy, and you make her happy, too. You are young, and mistakes come with being young and inexperienced. Don't let this make you complacent when it comes to intimacy. Just be careful and be the wonderful man I raised you to be," she said.

"Lily. Jack. I think you need to come down here," Jack's father called from the other room.

Jack followed his mother from the kitchen, the urgency in his father's voice spurring him forward. They came to a sudden halt at the sight of a very sheepish looking Mr. Hillman and a puffy-eyed Candice standing in the living room. Mr. Hillman still looked upset, but when he looked at Jack, his expression became almost grateful. Candice stood awkwardly at his side. She smiled carefully at him, and his heart knew everything would be okay.

"It's good to see you again, Candice," Lily said. "And you must be Candice's father, Mr. Hillman?" His mom stepped forward, her hand extended to shake Mr. Hillman's hand.

Jack knew that this wasn't the first time his mother had been forced to defuse a red-hot situation.

"Call me Damon, please. I'm sorry to arrive here unannounced, but I owe your son an apology." Mr. Hillman shifted from one foot to the other, decidedly uncomfortable.

Jack cautiously stepped forward, but his mother's hand on his arm stopped him. "Why don't we all sit down in the living room? Jack, why don't you and Candice go to the kitchen and fetch some coffee while your father and I talk to Damon."

Jack wanted to protest, but an expectant look thrown his way by his mom silenced any complaint.

"Candice." He held out his hand, and something inside him relaxed when her soft skin met his. Enjoying the thrilling sensation of her hand in his, he led Candice to the kitchen.

"I'm so sorry for my dad's behavior. I tried to reason with him, but I've never seen him so angry. I really thought he was going to hurt you," Candice whispered.

Jack tugged Candice into his arms again, grateful that he could hold her. He quickly collected all the makings for coffee, boiled the kettle, and with Candice's help, took them to the living room. His mom, dad, and Mr. Hillman talked in low tones in a close huddle of chairs. The voices drifted to silence as he and Candice entered.

"Uh . . . the coffee is ready," Jack said awkwardly. The tension in the room was palpable; He hoped his mom would be able to diffuse it without incident.

"I owe you an apology, Jack." Mr. Hillman stood from his chair and took the tray from Jack's hands, placing it on the coffee table. He extended his hand out to him. "I'm sorry. Candice explained the situation to me. She thinks the world of you, and she told me about all of the things you've done for her. My anger was unjustified and directed at the wrong person. Please accept my apology."

"Apology accepted, Mr. Hillman." Jack shook his hand firmly. "Please know that I think the world of Candice, too. I can't tell you how grateful I am that she came into my life, even under the circumstances."

Jack offered Mr. Hillman a smile and extended his arm out to Candice. She stepped in and cuddled into his side, and everyone sat down as Jack's mom poured coffee for the group.

"Damon, I'm not sure if Candice told you, but I work at a crisis pregnancy center in town. We spoke today about some options . . . " Jack's mom filled Mr. Hillman in on their discussion so far. Jack fazed out, concentrating on Candice and her warm fingers curled around his.

"I'm sorry," she said softly underneath the adult discussions.

"Hey, it's okay. I didn't think us being together would be easy. I'm here for you; you know that, right?" Jack said.

Candice nodded and settled back into his side. Jack glanced over at Mr. Hillman, and he felt an uneasiness growing within him. Over the course of the discussion, Mr. Hillman's friendly expression had grown darker and darker as Jack's mother explained what the pregnancy would mean for Candice and her future. At some point, Mr. Hillman seemed to come to a decision and nodded to himself. Jack didn't know why, but the sudden calmness in Mr. Hillman's expression caused a heavy weight to sink into the pit of his stomach.

When the coffee was finished, Mr. Hillman stood to his feet. "Come, Candice. I think it's time we should be going. Lily, John— thank you for your hospitality and your help. Lily, I appreciate all you've done for Candice."

"Dad, would it be okay if Jack brought me home in an hour?" Candice asked.

Mr. Hillman stiffened. He thought for a moment, his lips pursed, before he replied. "Okay. One hour, and no funny business."

Jack watched his mom go into full Mom Mode. "I assure you, Damon. Nothing like that goes on under my roof." Her implication was clear. Mr. Hillman had the grace to look ashamed.

He nodded and smiled. It was cordial, but it didn't reach his eyes. The unease in Jack's stomach grew. "I'll say goodnight then. Candice, one hour." He shook their hands and let himself out of the house.

The atmosphere relaxed as Mr. Hillman drove away. "That is one irate father. Be careful, my boy," Lily said.

"I'll be okay, Mom. My conscience is clear. Mr. Hillman will eventually figure out that he can trust me with Candice."

"In the current situation, it might take him a bit longer to accept you into her life." There was no mistaking the warning in his mom's words.

"I'll speak to him. He shouldn't treat you like that. It's not okay," Candice said.

Jack chuckled. "I'd like to see you try to defend me against your dad. He is a bit scary, especially when he's angry."

Lily smiled and patted her son on the arm. "Well then, we are off to bed. Good night, Candice. Jack, remember: one hour." His mom kissed his cheek, gave Candice a big hug, and then dragged his father upstairs, leaving them alone in the living room.

"I thought it was the end of us tonight," Jack said, pulling Candice down onto the sofa beside him. He shuddered at the thought of never seeing her again.

"Me, too. I know my dad. He's probably going to be irrational and overbearing for a while; but he'll probably go home tomorrow, and then everything will go back to normal," she said.

"I hope so." Jack kissed Candice's head and held her tighter. There had been something in Mr. Hillman's goodbye that had him worried. Maybe it was just his first introduction with Mr. Hillman that made him so on edge, but Jack really felt like there had been something off.

"So . . . about earlier," Candice said, her smile shy.

"Earlier?"

"When you kissed me."

Jack cheeks warmed. "About that . . . "

Candice laughed. "No complaints here."

"In that case . . . " Jack kissed her gently, sweetly, and then settled her against him. "Why don't we go to the den and watch something?" As much as he would have liked to stay there kissing her, he needed to be careful.

Candice nodded and they walked to the den together, settling in to watch some television. The act was so normal—so comfortable—that Candice felt like she could cry with relief. After all of the chaos of the last nine weeks of her life, she finally felt like she could be at peace.

One sitcom episode later, Jack pulled her from the sofa and stretched. "I should probably take you home. I don't want your dad making good on his threat."

Candice sighed. "You're probably right. We wouldn't want that."

Once they were in the car, Jack kissed her again, soft and chaste. He couldn't help himself. The nagging feeling that something bad was going to happen hadn't left, and he was desperate to be close to her.

Candice giggled. "Jack, the time."

"Okay, okay, we're going. I'm coming to fetch you for school tomorrow. I don't want you to have face Willow and her band of harpies or Brad alone."

He brought his car to a stop behind Mr. Hillman's dark blue SUV. The patio light blinked on.

Candice snorted. "Honestly, *now* my dad decides to worry?"

"I'll see you in the morning, beautiful." Jack kissed her quickly and hopped out of the car, running around to help her out and walk her to the door.

"Good night, Jack." She smiled so sweetly that he had to press down the urge to kiss her again.

"Good night, Candice. I'll see you tomorrow."

The words should have been easy for him to say. They were simple. Casual. So why did they stick in his throat? Why did he feel a sense of dread when he kissed her goodbye on the cheek and turned to leave? And why did his heart hammer and his stomach sink further with every step he took?

CHAPTER SEVENTEEN

Candice watched Jack walk back to his car, waiting until he was safely inside to close the front door of her house. She shut it with a giddy smile, feeling genuine happiness for the first time in a long time. Things were going well with Jack, and her dad was actually here. She'd been given a chance at a better life.

"I know, Andrea. I think . . . " her dad's voice dropped too low for her to hear what was said next. He ended his call and turned to her.

"Is everything okay?" Candice asked, but her smile quickly dropped when she saw the strange expression on her father's face.

Two cups of tea sat on the kitchen island, and an eerie silence filled the room. Mrs. Potter sat up with a start when she saw Candice. The small lines that formed around her mouth spelled out her distress.

"Did you have a nice time with Jack?" her father asked, but his tone made it clear that he didn't actually care one way or the other how her evening had gone.

Unease skated up her spine. Something was wrong.

"Yes, I did. Jack said he'd see me in the morning."

Mrs. Potter busied herself with the cups, her hands fidgeting in a way that made Candice nervous. Her father tapped the chair beside him, and Candice sat down, brows furrowed.

"Candice, I want to ask you something, and I need you to be very honest with me." There was an edge to her dad's voice. He sounded more upset than angry this time.

"O-okay."

"Is it true that your mother travels and works more than she's home?"

Candice shrugged, confused by the direction of the conversation. "Yeah. She stops in sometimes, typically just to pack another suitcase. But I'm used to it by now. It's okay."

"So, it's true that you've been practically raising yourself for the past few years?" Agitation crept into her father's voice.

She nodded. "I guess. Mrs. Potter's here to make sure I eat and stuff. At night, I make sure I lock the doors and activate the alarm. It's not such a big deal. I mean, I am almost eighteen."

His jaw clenched and the most heartbreaking look she'd ever seen appeared on her dad's face. He felt guilty. Candice knew her father tried to stay in her life, much more than her mother did, but since the divorce, the number of times their plans had worked out could be counted on two hands.

"Candice, why . . . why didn't you tell me? Every time I spoke to you, you never once mentioned you were alone so often or that your mother was away," he said.

"I didn't think anything of it. I mean, Mom hired Mrs. Potter, and she's almost always here," Candice said.

Harsh emotion flittered like a rollercoaster across her dad's features. He flew to his feet, pacing again. "This is unacceptable. No wonder you're in such a mess. You have too much freedom. You aren't ready to be responsible for yourself, let alone a baby."

"What are you saying, Dad?" Even as she asked the question, she knew the answer, and it wasn't good.

"You're coming back with me to Westwood. Tonight."

"No. Please, Dad, no," she begged, her voice barely audible even to her own ears.

"You obviously aren't getting the care and attention you need here, Candice. And as much as you love Mrs. Potter, she agrees with me. You need all the care you can get, especially now that you have a baby on the way."

"But, Dad, Jack and Lily are here to help me, not just Mrs. Potter. Besides, I've been fine so far!" Candice said desperately.

"Fine? You call this 'fine'? You are pregnant! At seventeen, Candice." He took a deep breath and clenched his fists. "I'm sorry, baby girl. I've made up my mind. You're going to stay with me until the baby is born and the adoption is done. And then, if you still want to, you can come back to Bethel and live with your mother until college."

This couldn't be happening. Tears ran in torrents down her cheeks. "What about Jack?"

At once, her father became contrite. "You are young. There will be other guys somewhere down the line."

A knife to the heart would have hurt less than what her father said. Although she'd been dancing with uncertainty over her emotions for Jack, when she thought of not seeing him again, her heart twisted painfully in her chest. Did she love him? Yes, she did. She loved everything about him. The way he laughed, the soft stroke of his mouth when he kissed her. The tenderness with how he treated her and the way he always stood by her as her protector. And now she wouldn't have the opportunity to tell him.

"Give me your phone and your laptop, please." Her father tapped the kitchen counter.

"What?" She locked her jaw, silencing the scream that bubbled up.

"This is for the best. I'm doing this to protect you, like your mother should have done a long time ago. Now, please go with Mrs. Potter and pack your things. You need a clean break," he said firmly.

"Daddy, please don't do this. My life is in Bethel," she begged. Ragged sobs built in her chest, heaving so hard her whole body shook.

Her father had aged in the past hours; the bright sunshine that used to fill his smile, the smile that brought her comfort and joy, was nowhere to be found. All that remained in its place was a hard-set line and ancient, green eyes. Resolute, her father held out his hand.

"Your phone, Candice."

He waited, staring at her until she slipped her phone from her pocket and handed it to him with trembling hands. He nodded and left the room, swiping her laptop from her backpack without a word.

Heartache shook her body as she climbed the wooden stairs to her room. She glanced over at Mrs. Potter and noticed the sorrow reflected in her own eyes. Silence hung like a dark cloud between them while they moved around her room, throwing clothes, shoes, and other random items into the large suitcases spread across her messy bed.

Her father waited just outside the doorway, her laptop tucked under one arm and her phone in his pocket. Her stomach clenched, and she swallowed, hoping it would stay her sadness. It didn't help; it continued to flow.

"I can't believe he's doing this," Candice said once her father had moved away from the door, busily talking on his phone. Probably calling her mom to yell at her.

Mrs. Potter sighed and zipped up the last suitcase. Her eyes were wet. She wiped them in a hurried movement and wrapped her in a hard hug. "I'm sorry, Candice. I don't agree with how your father is doing this, but it must be done. Your father wants to take care of you, and this, I think, is the best way he knows how. He loves you, Candice. Remember that."

There were no words to describe the turmoil of emotions inside Candice—the pain over her father's decision, the betrayal she felt as Mrs. Potter handed her over to her father, the despair of losing Jack and the realization that the little life inside her could feel it all. It was all too much. Her knees gave way beneath her, and she sank down onto the wooden floor, her body wanting to break into a million pieces from pain. She held it together with her arms.

"Quickly now, Candice. Your father wants to leave." Mrs. Potter tried to soothe her, her warm hand rubbing large circles on her bowed back. "I'm sorry," she whispered.

Numb, Candice allowed Mrs. Potter to pull her to her feet and guide her back down the stairs and into her father's car. There was nothing left to feel. Her eyes were dry as they left the town limits. Mile after mile, the car ate up the road, leaving behind the last four years.

Candice closed her eyes, praying that she would be able to breathe again. One lonely teardrop fell as she said a silent goodbye. To Jack, to Bethel, and to the only life she'd known.

CHAPTER EIGHTEEN

"What?" Jack's fist slammed into the door frame with a sickening thud. Jack didn't feel any pain—the devastation brought on by Mrs. Potter's words overshadowed it.

"I'm sorry, Jack," Mrs. Potter said softly. Her voice was fragile, and her eyes were filled with pity. "Candice's dad took her home with him. She won't be coming back."

This can't be happening.

There had to be a way he could see her. He *needed* to see her.

"Can I call her?" he asked desperately.

Before Mrs. Potter could answer, Jack had already dialed Candice's number. The call connected, and he could hear her ringtone play from somewhere in the house. His heart sank.

"I'm sorry, Jack. You won't be able to call or contact her. Her father thinks she needs a new start—to focus on finishing school and having her baby. Please try to understand; it's what she needs."

"But . . . " Jack's protest died on his lips, his mind spinning in circles.

Did Mr. Hillman think he wasn't good enough for his daughter? Memories from the night before scrolled through his mind. Mr. Hillman's face when he'd left. The sinking feeling in his stomach. His gut had been right. When Mr. Hillman and Candice had come to

Jack's house, he had already made his mind up. He hadn't been there to reconcile, although his apology looked genuine. He'd been there to let Candice say goodbye.

They just hadn't known it would be permanent.

Jack squeezed the bridge of his nose between his thumb and forefinger and took deep, even breaths. Losing his cool wouldn't help anyone.

Mrs. Potter held up her hand, her grief as clear as day. "Please leave, Jack. There is nothing for you here." A solitary tear slid down her soft and downy cheek. Her small hand trembled as she squeezed his. "I'm sorry. But if you really care about her, then you'll do what is best for her and the baby."

And with those whispered words, Mrs. Potter closed the door, leaving Jack standing on the porch.

I love her.

With wooden legs, Jack walked to the car and slid in, staring out the window and seeing nothing. Then, he began to cry.

Why don't they understand?

Burying his head in his hands, he gasped for breath as sobs wracked his body, shaking his tall frame. Candice was gone, and he didn't know where she was. The thought brought a new wave of despair, pressing against his chest so heavily that he was sure his heart would crack.

I love her. Help us.

He didn't know how long he sat outside her house. He didn't know where else to go. The only thing he *could* do was pray.

Bright sunlight and the smell of seawater did nothing to lift the gray cloud hanging over Candice's head. The new living arrangements were strange and uncomfortable. It was stifling being supervised twenty-four hours a day, seven days a week. Her father's constant hovering was driving her crazy. "Candice, have you eaten? Candice, have you showered today? What about the baby, Candice?" She could scream. Two weeks. It had been two weeks since she'd last seen Jack. Two weeks of begging and pleading, to no avail. Her dad was immovable.

Candice threw her math textbook across the desk and sighed, rubbing her eyes roughly. The numbers had begun to blur together about ten minutes ago, but study hours were the only time her dad let her be alone. Tonight had not been a particularly good night. They'd gotten into a fight about Jack again.

Candice's eyes drifted over to the shiny new laptop laying on her bed. Her dad had bought it solely for her schoolwork, and she knew he was closely monitoring its use. But still . . . There was always the option to erase her search history.

What if . . .

She snagged the laptop, an idea forming in her head. The screen came alive as soon as she touched the keyboard, and she hastily pulled up the search engine page. She typed "Save a Life Pregnancy Center" into the search bar and scanned the results, hoping that Lily's number might be listed somewhere on the website.

Her breath caught in her throat when she saw Lily Anson's phone number on the "Contact Us" page. Candice grabbed her phone—also brand new and empty of any contacts, other than her dad and Mrs. Potter—and dialed the number with trembling fingers.

The phone rang.

She had to see him. She just wanted to say she was sorry, and she wanted to tell him how she felt. The words had been there all along, although they had never come out. She wrapped her arms around herself and hoped that she could hold herself together.

"Hello, this is the Save a L—"

Candice felt her phone being ripped away from her ear.

"Candice, who are you talking to?" Her dad loomed over her, his gaze darting to her computer screen and back to her phone. His jaw hardened. Without a word, he ended the call and collected her laptop, taking both her phone and computer with him.

Anger burned through her. She grabbed the nearest stack of books and flung them across the room until there was nothing left to do but curl up in a ball and cry. Before darkness took her, she lay a trembling hand on her stomach, stroking the small, growing bump with her fingertips.

"I'm sorry, baby," Candice said, her voice rough from her tears. As she felt the bump, she remembered the thrumming sound of her baby's heartbeat in the Save a Life Center all those weeks ago. "What are we going to do?"

Westwood was an enchanting, small coastal town where a sparkling, blue sea lapped on the edge of a white and brown sandy shore. It was beautiful and warm. The bright sun lightly burned Candice's skin, replacing the coldness that invaded her body since moving away from Bethel. The slight headache that remained from last night's crying fit was slowly disappearing as she breathed in the fresh, salty air around her.

Her father had forced her to come to the beach today.

"Baby girl, you're in one of the most beautiful places in the country. Go outside for a while," he had said. "Go swim in the sea, get a tan, and enjoy the nature around us. Besides, I don't think all this moping is good for you or the baby."

The baby. That was always what it came down to. Some days, Candice wondered if her dad worried more about her unborn child than her. She sighed again. The slight protrusion of her belly barely showed underneath her floral tank top. If a person were to look at her, they would never guess that she was carrying a life in her stomach. The sand cupped her elbows as she leaned back on the shoreline. Here, breathing in the stillness, Candice was able to find a small measure of peace.

In the days following her departure from Bethel, Candice worked to strengthen the connection she'd made with God that day at the center. On her first day in Westwood, she'd found a beautiful leather-bound Bible while unpacking. It had a single name written neatly on the inside of the cover: Matilda Potter. At first, she'd wanted to hurl the book into the nearest trash can, but the part of Candice that still loved Mrs. Potter, despite her perceived betrayal, stopped her. Candice grew to treasure that Bible as if it was her only lifeline. When the nights were dark and the days were long, the soothing words gave her the peace and comfort she so desperately sought and reminded her of a love that surpassed everything. Psalms was her favorite book. In each verse and chapter, she read of triumph, suffering, and the mercy and love of God.

Wiping at her eyes, Candice picked up her Bible from beside her and began to read Psalm 23:

The Lord is my shepherd, I lack nothing.
He makes me lie down in green pastures,

he leads me beside quiet waters,
he refreshes my soul.
He guides me along the right paths
for his name's sake.
Even though I walk
through the darkest valley,
I will fear no evil,
for you are with me;
your rod and your staff,
they comfort me.

You prepare a table before me
in the presence of my enemies.
You anoint my head with oil;
my cup overflows.
Surely your goodness and love will follow me
all the days of my life,
and I will dwell in the house of the Lord forever.

It was a well-loved Psalm and a comfort to her in her time of desperation. She bowed her head, silently giving words to the pain in her heart.

Opening her eyes, she let her gaze wander over the blue expanse of sea in front of her and smiled. Her baby was growing well. Her ever-present morning sickness was testimony enough for that. Her father had scheduled another appointment with the doctor to see how the baby was growing. She'd read somewhere that the sicker she was in the first months of pregnancy, the more assurance she could have over the health and well-being of her baby.

Her phone buzzed beside her, catching her attention. It was Mrs. Potter again. She ignored the call, watching it go to voicemail. A watch could be set by the times Mrs. Potter called. Twice a day. Once at ten in the morning and again at four in the afternoon. Candice ignored each call. She had nothing to say to Mrs. Potter.

And then there was her mother. Candice's ears still stung from the tongue-lashing her mother had unleashed on her father when she had finally returned from her business trip. The call had been on speaker, not that it bothered her mother much. Seeing the devastation on Candice's face, her father had eventually agreed to speak to her elsewhere and took the phone with him when he left the room. She was supposed to come next week to "check on Candice."

I won't hold my breath.

Another wave collided with the wet sand. The dark print left on the clean shore dampened her peaceful mood. Thinking of her mom often did that. So did thinking of Jack. She tried not to, but it seemed almost impossible. Every time she saw someone with his color hair, build, or those blue eyes that resembled the sea, her heart rate sped up, and she would gasp for breath. She missed Jack. Missed him terribly.

Pages fluttered in the afternoon breeze, and Candice read the Psalm again. The words helped. They always did. For now, it was all she had.

CHAPTER NINETEEN

It was graduation day, and Jack was not in the headspace to celebrate. School had become a playground of noise and colors. If his mom hadn't told him today was the last time he'd walk the halls of Bethel Private School, he wouldn't have known. It was like he was looking in on something of which he wasn't a part. One person was glaringly absent today: Candice.

Once the ceremony had passed him by, Jack sat on his bed beside Christian. He looked about as bad as Jack did. This day had been hard for him, too—just for different reasons.

"How you are doing, man?" Christian asked.

Jack shrugged. "About the same, I guess. No worse, no better. I tried to call Mrs. Potter again—still no news. She refused to tell me if Candice was at least okay."

Christian nodded. "I'm sorry, man. But it will work out, I'm sure of it. God has a plan . . . I just wish I knew what it was."

"How can you still be so sure?" Jack asked. Christian's dogged faith was something Jack battled to understand, especially over the last months. Willow, once the queen witch of Bethel, had changed almost miraculously. After she'd matured, she had become Christian's girlfriend, but then she'd been involved in a brutal car accident, which left Christian devastated and Willow in a coma. Jack didn't know how Christian coped some days.

A sudden fervor overtook Christian, his eyes blazing to life. "I know how this is going to sound to you, but despite how you feel right now—despite what has happened—God still loves you. He knows what He's doing with Willow and yes, with Candice too. I don't have the answers, and I wish I did, but I do know the One who does. Trust in the Lord, Jack. Take everything to Him in prayer. He'll help. He wants to help."

Jack nodded. He admired Christian's dedication, and he wanted to feel as secure and sure as Christian did. But how?

It was late in the night when Jack finally pulled himself off the couch and walked to his room. Christian had left hours ago and returned to the hospital that had become his second home since Willow's accident.

Weaving his fingers behind his head, Jack lay down on his bed, his heart sore. His eyes slid shut of their own accord, and a still, small voice whispered into the emptiness.

Trust Me.

Jack's breath caught. He waited. Listened.

Trust Me.

A thick wall of emotion, hardened by months of pain, split down the middle, light bursting into the darkness. Hope that had been so absent for a long time filled the emptiness. Jack leaped from his bed and fell to his knees, head buried in his hands. No words came to him except the ones crying from his soul.

God, help me.

It was time to move on with his life. Over the next month, he went to church with Christian, studied his Bible, and little by little, Jack's broken heart began to heal. Inch by painful inch, Jack climbed out of the dark pit he'd been in since Candice had left. His faith became an important part of him, but it did not take away the questions. Questions that made him sick to his stomach. Had it been Mr. Hillman's idea to leave, or had Candice wanted it, too?

He needed a change. A new start. Something that would help him get away from the memories for a while. Naturally, an opportunity presented itself the very next day.

"Jack, are you busy?" his mom asked.

"Not really." Jack looked up from the stack of papers in front of him: college applications for the following school year. Extremely late applications.

"I had a thought. There is an old friend of mine, Doris Huntsman, in a small town called Westwood about five hours from here. She mentioned that she was opening her house to young house guests for the summer. I thought you might like to go and maybe clear your head before college. It might do you a world of good."

"Are you and Dad just trying to get rid of me for the summer?" he teased.

His mother grinned. "You're onto us. No, seriously, though. I think it's a great opportunity for you. Ask Christian! He might want to go, too."

"Sure, Mom. I'll do that." He could use a change of scenery, and he was sure Christian could, too.

The glow of morning had just broken as Jack and Christian loaded up the car.

"Jack, I don't know about this. I mean . . . " Christian trailed off.

Jack's heart broke for Christian and the struggle he faced. It had been months since Willow's accident, and Christian rarely left her side. Jack admired Christian's persistent hope, but as the time bled on, Christian's hope was fading.

"Look, man, I know you're worried, but think about it. When Willow wakes up, she's going to need you twenty-four hours a day for who knows how long. Take this time to just chill; you need it. It can't do any harm," Jack said.

Christian threw his bag in the trunk and slunk into the passenger seat. His body was stiff with tension.

"I know it's hard, but try to relax, man. We've got a long drive ahead of us," Jack said.

Five hours later, long stretches of sparkling ocean and glorious beach greeted them. The sun hung high, and the damp heat wrapped around them like a warm blanket. Jack grinned at Christian, feeling genuinely happy for the first time in a long time. Over the course of the drive, Christian gradually relaxed, the pinched expression he'd worn for months dissolving into one that resembled a time before all the stuff with Willow had happened.

They continued driving around the outskirts of Westwood toward Mrs. Huntsman's house. He brought the car to a stop outside of the small cottage. It was cute, white, and surrounded by every colored flower known to man. The view from the house revealed a stretch of sand and the big blue openness of the ocean. He could picture himself out there amongst the waves, laughing as he and Christian tried to surf. Coming here was a good choice.

Jack and Christian climbed out of the car, the humidity sticking their shirts to their backs.

"Nice place," Jack said.

A group of girls dressed for the beach walked past them, giggling and waving. Jack politely waved back, and Christian ignored them.

With a loud smack, the front door opened, and an older lady dressed in nautical fashion walked down the patio toward them. Her smile reminded Jack of his mom's, and he instantly felt at home.

"Jack and Christian. Is that right? I'm Doris Huntsman, but you can just call me Doris."

She dragged Jack into a hug and then did the same with Christian.

Ms. Doris sized the two boys up, and Jack saw a twinkle in her kind, blue eyes.

"Come on in and get comfortable. The heat is dreadful today. I'm sure you boys are tired after your long journey," she said.

Jack sighed. That was an understatement. His journey hadn't started five hours ago; no, his journey had started some months ago the day he'd run into Candice at the park. And now, he was ready for it to end and a new one to begin.

"Thank you for offering your home to us, we appreciate it," he said warmly.

Doris's expression became sympathetic. "I understand both you boys have had a difficult few months. I know how lost I felt after my husband passed on and went to be with the Lord. I wished I had some place to go, just to retreat for a while with the cares of the world forgotten. When I chatted with your mother, I knew this would be the perfect place for you two."

Jack nodded. He saw Christian do the same out of the corner of his eye. Mrs. Doris smiled kindly. "You've come to the right place, boys. Westwood is a lovely place to relax and replenish." She ushered them through the door with a welcoming air.

Cool air met them as they walked through the open door. Doris's house was charming. Sailor-themed decor flowed effortlessly from the sunny front room to the kitchen and upstairs.

"You boys are up here." Doris showed them to two bedrooms at the top of the stairs, one on either side. A large room sat between the other two: Doris's room.

"Jack, you can take the left room, and Christian you can take the right. When you boys have settled in, come downstairs. I'm going to make some lunch," she said.

"Thank you," the boys chorused.

Jack admired the photos that ran the length of the hallway. The pictures showed Doris smiling wide, surrounded by a large family, possibly her children. In another photo, a man about the same age as Doris gazed into her eyes. Her husband. The two were obviously in love. He grimaced as memories twisted his heart. He pushed them away. New start.

He tossed his bag on the floor, deciding that food was far more important than unpacking. He walked down the hall to Christian's room and popped his head in.

"You ready to get some food?" Jack asked.

"Just about," Christian said, putting another shirt in the dresser drawer. "How can you be done so quickly?"

"Priorities. I'm starving."

Christian rolled his eyes. "Some things never change. Okay, neanderthal. Let's get down there."

The sound of a knife chopping vegetables greeted them as they entered the kitchen. Doris stood behind a large, white marble island in the middle of the kitchen, surrounded by white cabinets and a nice-looking oven.

"Come in, come in. I'm almost done. Do you want to help me with the peppers, Jack? And, Christian, if you don't mind, can you get the chicken out of the icebox? I hope chicken salad sandwiches are okay."

"Jack eats anything, and I'm partial to those." Christian's eager smile gave Jack hope that Christian was feeling a bit better than when they'd left that morning.

Doris chatted all throughout lunch about the festivals and various happenings that went on during the summer in Westwood and which ones she thought Christian and Jack should attend. In record time, Jack and Christian had polished off the stack of sandwiches Doris had made.

"My, my! I'd almost forgotten how much young men eat. Are you sure you've had enough?" she fretted.

"Yes, thank you, Mrs. Doris. That was wonderful," Jack assured. Christian nodded happily in agreement, his hand resting on his full stomach.

They excused themselves from the table; it was time to explore.

CHAPTER TWENTY

Mid-July brought the tourist season to Westwood. Candice wiggled her now-sizeable stomach between the tables at Daisy's Diner. Her baby boy kicked wildly, bouncing like a little monkey inside her. A few weeks ago, she had received her high school diploma and a clean bill of health for her and her baby. In celebration, her father had thrown a small dinner party for himself; Candice; Candice's boss, Daisy; and Daisy's daughter, Rose. In between the ice cream cake and balloons, she'd insisted it was time for her to get a job, despite her dad's protests. He worried incessantly. Each night, her dad would tell her another horror story of teenage pregnancy that he had read online. She didn't know if he was trying to make sure she didn't get pregnant ever again or if he was genuinely worried about her.

Daisy was a Godsend. Her daughter was the product of a teenage pregnancy, too, and Candice had spent many hours talking with Daisy and listening to her advice. Daisy had become a good friend and often gave her a safe place to go and cry when the thoughts of Jack became too much. Lately, those moments were more and more distant. As impactful and intense as her weeks with Jack had been, it was time for her to look to the future. Jack was no longer in her life, and she doubted he thought about her much anymore. He was probably playing college basketball and dreaming about a future in the NBA. He didn't have time to think of an ex-girlfriend, friend, or whatever she'd been to him.

Stop it, Candice.

Today, her thoughts seemed adamant to stay on Jack. Annoyed, Candice slammed the salt and pepper shakers onto the table with more force than necessary.

"Trouble?" Daisy asked. She was a few years younger than Candice's mother, and her long, black hair was tied in a messy bun at the back of her head. Her hazel eyes focused on Candice.

"No, just having a mourning moment," Candice said. "Mourning moment" was the phrase they used when Candice was really struggling. Daisy understood what it meant.

"Hang in there. It takes time," Daisy said with a sympathetic smile.

A customer ambled into the diner, and Candice rushed over to help.

"Daisy's Diner. What can I get for you?" she asked brightly.

The lady looked just like Mrs. Potter, except for the bright red lipstick and floral hat. Mrs. Potter's clothes were usually muted colors; her lipstick was typically a pale pink. An uncomfortable mix of emotions surged up in Candice. Mrs. Potter had kept her father's commands faultlessly. Each time Candice begged for news of Jack, Mrs. Potter had refused and always gave the same reason. Her dad had asked her not to. All of Candice's tears and pleading had yielded nothing.

Two months ago, Candice had asked again, and the answer was the same. That was the last time she'd spoken to Mrs. Potter. She'd never admit it to anyone, but that decision had brought on its own set of tears.

Candice swallowed hard as she took the lady's order, her New England accent nothing like the American/Italian accent Mrs. Potter spoke with, and it made her heart ache.

By the end of her shift, her feet ached, and her baby boy seemed to be having a party inside her belly. His constant movements made it almost impossible to spend more than thirty minutes away from a washroom. Candice ran her hand tenderly over her stomach, love spreading like warmth around her. She hoped her son looked more like her than Brad, more for the baby's sake than her own. It was strange to think of Brad now and how he would not have any part in his baby's life. And then there was Jack. A tear leaked out before she could stop it. She forced a smile and tried to shift her thoughts away from Jack, praying for the peace she'd sought so often lately. God was her Rock, and with His help and strength, her heart would heal.

Candice sat down in a single seater sofa in the employee lounge, propped her feet up on the nearby coffee table, and closed her eyes to pray.

Lord, please help me. I can't do it today. It's too hard.

"Let's do something fun tonight," Rose whispered in her ear, interrupting her prayer.

Candice jumped, startled. "The only thing I want right now is a hot bath and chocolate fudge ice cream. Why, what do you want to do?"

Rose squealed. Oh, to be seventeen and that enthusiastic. Being pregnant had aged Candice beyond her years, and she'd lost most of her enthusiasm for life.

"There's a huge party at the beach tonight!" Rose said. "Everyone will be there. Maybe you can meet someone and get over whatever-his-name-is back home."

Candice sighed; perhaps Rose was right. She didn't want another relationship right now, though. After all, what teenage boy would want an obviously pregnant girlfriend?

Jack wanted you.

She pushed the thought away. But still, some more friends her own age would be nice.

"Sure," Candice said. "That sounds like a great idea."

"Great! Find something to wrap that gorgeous body in, and I'll pick you up at five," Rose said.

"It's a sin to lie, Rose," Candice quipped as Rose disappeared out of the room.

She sighed. Rose and Candice were almost the same age, except Rose would be off to college in the fall and Candice would be a mother. That thought alone made her spirit sink.

Maybe it really was time. Maybe she'd meet someone tonight and begin the journey of forgetting Jack Anson. Maybe tonight would be the beginning of something great.

CHAPTER TWENTY-ONE

"Heads up!" someone shouted from the beach.

Jack turned his head just in time to see a white volleyball hurtling toward him and Christian. Jack caught it quickly and noticed a group of young people jogging over to talk to them.

"This yours?" Jack asked.

A tall teen with fuzzy, brown hair walked over. He reminded Jack of a stuffed bear he'd had when he was little. "Yeah, man. You and your friend want to play? We're a couple of guys short today," he said.

"Sure! You up for it?" Jack asked Christian.

"Definitely," Christian said.

"Awesome. I'm Matt, by the way. The other two clowns over there are Ben and Tyler," Matt said, leading them over to a makeshift volleyball net.

"I'm Jack, and this is Christian," Jack said.

"Nice to meet you," Christian said to the boys.

"Same to you. What brings you to Westwood?" Matt lobbed the ball over the net, seemingly unconcerned in which direction it went. It flew over neatly and landed with a decisive thud between the other guys.

"Summer," Jack said simply. He watched Christian stifle a grin beside him.

"So, you're tourists, then?"

"Not sure yet." The truth was that Jack didn't really know what would happen. College was waiting, yet there was something telling him that Westwood was where he was meant to be. He couldn't explain it. Maybe he should think about getting a job. He didn't want to be a weight on Ms. Doris's shoulders if he needed to stay longer. He and Christian had discussed it over the past few days. For some reason, Westwood felt like home.

The sand was warm under his feet as Jack took position behind the net between Christian and Matt. Ben and Tyler faced off against them. Matt served, and the game was on. Small droplets of sweat slid down his back. Their team was three points ahead. Tyler and Ben were playing with a boisterous fervor as they fought to take back the lead. It was Jack's turn to serve. He lobbed the ball into the air, and his hand met the white leather with a satisfying smack as the ball sailed over the net. One, two, three, and the game was over. Jack's team emerged the unquestionable victors.

Matt high-fived Jack and Christian. "You guys aren't half-bad. By the way, if you're down to hang out later, there's a party tonight at the beach. You two should come," Matt said.

"Nah, maybe not tonight. I'm beat," Christian said.

"Come on, it'll be fun. Nothing better to do on a summer's night than hang out with a babe and a bonfire on the beach," Tyler said, playfully pumping his biceps.

"Christian has a girlfriend back home, but I'm up for it," Jack said.

"Great! Where are you guys staying?" Matt asked.

"Over at Doris Huntsman's house."

"Ah, the old lady with the great pies. I know her. The party starts at five. If you drink anything but pop, bring it with you. If not, there is a bar there. I can come and get you later just before five," Matt said.

"Sounds like a plan," Jack said.

After the group parted ways, Christian walked beside Jack, seemingly lost in thought. When they reached the car, Jack opened his door and was stunned to see someone who looked like Candice across the road.

Your mind is just playing tricks on you, man.

Candice was always on his mind—he'd just gotten better at ignoring the pain. He climbed into the car and dismissed the girl. There was no way she would be in Westwood of all places.

"Are you okay?" Christian asked, sliding into the car beside him.

Jack shrugged off his concern.

"Just come to the beach and hang out," Jack said. "I know you don't really want to, but just for tonight, can you be my wingman?"

With some reluctance, Christian agreed. Jack shook his head sympathetically; he hurt for Christian. Although the desolate look was gone, he still worried so much. "She'll be okay, man. Keep praying," Jack said.

"I do," Christian whispered.

The journey back to the cottage was silent. Jack watched Christian as he walked into the house. With hunched shoulders, he climbed the stairs and gently closed his bedroom door behind him. Jack sighed. Christian was probably going to call his mom and check in on Willow.

"Jack, is that you?" Mrs. Doris called from the kitchen. "Are you boys hungry?"

"Yep, let me go and ask Christian if he wants something to eat." Jack ran up the stairs and knocked on Christian's door.

"No news?" Jack asked as he opened it.

"No change," Christian said dully.

"Come on, let's get something to eat," Jack said, giving Christian an encouraging pat on the back.

"Sure, I'm starving." A hint of a grin lifted Christian's cheek. Jack smiled in return. For now, Christian would be okay.

Doris had outdone herself for lunch today. Two huge hamburgers with all the fixings were on the kitchen island waiting for them.

"Ms. Doris, you shouldn't let us take advantage of you like this," Jack said. He sat down, and his mouth watered at the delicious sight on his plate.

"Nonsense! You boys have become like my own, and I can spoil you if I want. Now, if you'll excuse me, I have a bridge game at Molly's house." Molly was as old as the hills and Doris's neighbor. The two of them were never far from a bridge game or each other.

"We're going to a party tonight. We will probably be back late," Jack said.

"Okay, boys. Be careful." Doris kissed both boys on their cheeks and walked out the door in a whirl of white linen and floral perfume.

Christian grinned at Jack, and they both dug into their food. After they cleaned up the dishes for Ms. Doris, they went to get ready for the party. Jack threw on his favorite pair of dark jeans and a pale blue t-shirt. His heart drummed unevenly in his chest. Why was he suddenly so nervous?

Maybe because you've been a recluse for four months, genius.

Jack heard a car honk outside, and he and Christian rushed out of the house and piled into Matt's truck. The drive wasn't long, but Jack felt his anticipation rising with every second.

A pleasant thrill buzzed through his veins as he and Christian climbed out of the car. They followed Matt down to the beach, where a large group was gathered by a roaring bonfire. Music and voices floated up to them from further down the beach, and couples danced and laughed, kicking up sand as they went. A few teens sat on long logs pulled close to the fire to form seats.

"Hey, you guys made it! Welcome. The bar is over there; grab something and join us," Ben said.

"I'll think I'll just hang out over here," Christian said. He sat down on one of the logs and was soon engaged in a conversation with a couple sitting beside him. Jack smiled at the scene, happy to see Christian participating. He grabbed a can of soda from the bar and walked down to where Matt and Tyler stood with a group of people.

"Everyone, this is Jack. Jack, this is everyone," Matt said.

"Thanks for the intro," Jack said with a laugh.

A blonde girl with a brilliant smile caught his eye and turned to him. "Hi, Jack. I'm Amber. So, you're a friend of Matt's?"

Jack shrugged noncommittally. "I guess. We only met today at the beach. I'm kind of visiting Westwood for the summer."

Jack and Amber slowly started to migrate away from the group and closer to the fire.

"Well, welcome. You've come at the best time of year," Amber said, sitting down on one of the logs by the fire.

"So I've heard. Is it always this hot?" he asked, sitting next to her. This girl was nice to talk to, and the music mixed with the evening breeze made him feel at ease for the first time in a while.

"Yep. Every summer," she said.

"I gather you're a local?" he asked.

"Born and raised. My dad owns the hardware store in town," she said.

"That's cool," Jack said. Then, he heard a familiar song begin to play, and he just couldn't help himself. He wanted to let loose, just a bit. "Would you like to dance?" he asked boldly.

Amber's smile got brighter. A small spark of attraction ran through Jack when she laid her hand on his and pulled him to his feet. "I would love to," she said.

They danced again and again till both were panting. "I need a break," Amber gasped and lifted her wet hair off her neck. "Do you want a water?"

"Yeah, thanks. I just need to check on someone, too," Jack said.

"A girl someone?" she asked.

Jack chuckled. "No, actually, my friend came with me. He's been going through a bit of a rough time."

"Oh, I'm sorry. Do you think he'll be okay?"

"Yeah, I hope with time he will be."

Jack scanned the crowd for Christian's familiar black hair. His eyes trailed over the crowd and onto the shoreline. Then, he noticed something that made him pause. There, in the shadow of a nearby palm tree, was a figure. There was something about the figure that made him stand up and take notice. It was as if he knew the figure—a girl. He was drawn to her like a moth to a flame. The sight of her beckoned him like someone from his dreams. His heart thrashed.

Could it be?

The party faded into the background. The figure turned, and her auburn hair glowed in the setting sun, a bump protruding from the folds of her dark dress. The dying light of the sun lit her face. So dear to him. Jack's breath caught in his chest. Her warm, brown eyes collided with his, the same disbelief that shook his frame reflected in them.

"Jack, are you okay?" Amber asked, her words sounding muffled to his ears.

"I'm sorry, Amber. I . . . I have to go." Dazed, he didn't hear her reply.

Then, he ran to her. Candice.

CHAPTER TWENTY-TWO

The sound of waves rushing the shore lured Candice to the water's edge.

Why did I come here?

All around her were kids her own age, living life, not responsible for anyone but themselves. Innocent. Her baby kicked again.

"It's okay. We're okay," she said.

It seemed like second nature for her to run her hand over her baby bump now. The thought of having a baby didn't scare her so much anymore. Another wave lapped the shore, and a thin stream of water snuck all the way up to the dry sand and spilled over it. She followed the trail of water, her eyes slowly sweeping back up to the party. And then, she froze. Her heart seized, and she gasped.

"Jack?"

He was staring at her. Just staring. As if she held the sun in her hands.

He said something to a girl standing beside him. Then, he ran to her. One moment he was across the beach; and the next, he was kicking up sand, panting and staring and towering over Candice.

"Candice," he whispered, his hands cupping her face, making sure she was real.

"Jack." Her hands found his warm chest. "Jack."

Warm hands ran tenderly up her arms and banded around her back. His lips met hers. The kiss was as soft as a breath. "Candice." And then, he kissed her again. Long, slow, and tender. His pent-up emotion showed in each sweep of his mouth.

"Why didn't you contact me?" The warmth of the moment before was gone, replaced by bitter cold. Jack pulled back and crossed his arms over his chest, his posture hard and unrelenting and clearly showing his feelings of hurt. "Why, Candice? Why didn't you tell me where you'd gone?"

"I couldn't," she said desperately. "My dad—"

"Let me guess, he didn't think I was good enough for you?" Jack said.

"No! I don't know. But that's not . . . " Tears gathered in the corners of her eyes, and her throat closed from emotion. Candice had dreamed about seeing Jack again countless times; but in all those dreams, she'd never imagined him angry with her.

"Jack," she pleaded. Her hands reached for him, but Jack stepped back. Why hadn't she told him how she felt when she'd had the chance?

"Was it all a game to you? You find a sympathetic guy to keep you company until your dad came to the rescue?" No words came to her in the face of his wrath. "It was, wasn't it? You know what, I'm done. I'm over it. I won't be the fool again." He took a deep pull of air, pain bleeding into his words. "Goodbye, Candice."

"No, Jack, he took everything!" Her words didn't reach him. He was already on his way back toward the fire, his long legs eating up the sand in quick, resentful steps.

Another wave washed over her bare feet, and the cold tingle brought her back to herself. All the pain and sorrow she'd thought she'd gotten over roared back to life, and her heart broke again. She watched as Jack spoke to his friend Christian, and the two quickly disappeared into the dark night. Her tears spilled over and ran down her cheeks. She tasted their salty wetness on her lips.

"Candice, are you okay?" Rose asked appearing out of the darkness. "Candice?"

"He's here," she murmured.

"Who's here?"

"The boy I love." She covered her eyes with her hands and sobbed. "I thought . . . I thought . . . " Her words were lost in a river of tears.

"Ah, honey," Rose soothed softly. "He seems like a real jerk."

Why had he said those words? And kissed her like his life depended on it?

"Come on, I'm taking you home," Rose said.

Candice let Rose lead her to the car, shattered all over again.

Pain ripped into Jack. Candice stood silent, eyes wide and tearful. Her expression was confused. Her eyes silently pleaded with him to understand.

Don't be fooled, Jack.

The angry beast inside him quashed any sympathy he may have felt. All he could feel was hurt. Clenching his hands, he crossed the beach to Christian and left Candice behind.

"Dude, we're leaving."

"You okay, man?" he asked.

Jack shuddered. "Fine. You ready to go?"

Christian nodded. "Yeah, all good."

Jack didn't bother with goodbyes. Right now, he wasn't good company for anyone. The long walk back to the house was silent. The beast reared its head again and again. His frustration grew with each step.

His mattress sagged underneath his weight as he threw himself onto it.

Lord, what's going on?

His heart hurt so much that it reverberated throughout his entire body. Why didn't he feel happy? He'd finally found Candice after all this time, yet her leaving had created more betrayal and resentment in him than he realized. He'd come all this way to find peace and a new start; instead, he'd run smack into the past and the pain he was so sure he'd left behind. For many hours, Jack just stared at the ceiling, Candice's pleading expression haunting him.

"Candice, are you okay?" The footrest of the recliner smacked back into place as her father flew out of his chair.

"I'm fine." She pushed past him and ran up to her room. It was his fault. All his fault. If he hadn't made her leave Bethel the way he had and taken everything from her, she and Jack would be together, and she wouldn't be feeling this terrible anguish. Another wave of emotion hit, forcing her onto her knees beside her bed.

God, where are You?

Mrs. Potter's face instantly appeared in her mind, and her unresolved forgiveness issues stared her in the face. God couldn't help if she refused to forgive Mrs. Potter. After all, Mrs. Potter was as much a victim to her father's demands as Candice was.

I've been so blind.

Her hands trembled as she fumbled for her phone and dialed a number.

"Candice? Are you all right? Do you know what time it is?" Mrs. Potter picked up immediately, her words flowing with anxious fervor.

"Mrs. Potter. Oh, I'm so sorry. I didn't think. I just . . . I just needed to speak to someone."

"Of course, dear. I know you are angry with me, but I'm always here for you."

"Mrs. Potter, I'm so sorry. I'm stupid and childish, and I'm not angry with you. I miss you so much. Please forgive me," Candice begged.

"Already done, dear," she soothed. "Now, what is the matter?"

"Jack is here."

"In Westwood?" Mrs. Potter tone rose in pitch with surprise.

"Yes. I saw him tonight on the beach. Mrs. Potter, he's so angry. I'm sure he hates me," Candice sobbed.

"He was here about a week ago, and I'm sure that isn't the case. The hopeless boy I saw was someone who was still desperately attached to you. I considered just telling him where you were to put him out of his misery. I'm sorry, too. I wouldn't have agreed if I'd known what this would do to you and Jack," Mrs. Potter said.

"I don't know what to do. I love him." It was the first time she'd said the words out loud. As soon as they had crossed her tongue, she'd known they were still true.

"The only thing left to do is to pray. I'll pray for you and Jack. Leave it with God, Candice. He is the only One Who can fix this problem. God brought Jack to Westwood for a reason, and we need to trust Him and His purpose."

"Mrs. Potter, I missed you so much."

"I missed you, too, dear. Now, tell me, how are you? And how is the baby?"

The next hour was spent laughing and crying together. A freedom that Candice had missed lifted the weight of bitterness off her shoulders. She felt at peace. A relationship was renewed from the forgiveness received. The floorboards creaked under her knees as she knelt again. She closed her eyes and bowed her head over her clasped hands.

Dear Lord . . .

After she had spent time in prayer, she rose to climb into her bed and felt confident that God would handle the situation with Jack if she let Him.

Her heart still throbbed painfully, but overriding the pain was the sweet, soothing feeling of hope. The gentle kicks in her belly seemed to feel that hope, too.

CHAPTER TWENTY-THREE

The light of another morning did nothing to ease the ache in Jack's heart. The gentle crash of the waves and the sunrise over their azure depths didn't bring the peace he craved.

Candice, Candice, Candice.

Her name drummed with each beat of his heart. He was head over heels for her, and the lie he'd managed to convince himself of was nothing but that—a lie. His heart had never let go of her. A long jog didn't get rid of her face from his memory, and the long shower after couldn't erase her kisses from his heart.

"Good morning, Jack." Mrs. Doris said, chipper as usual.

"Morning. Where's Christian?" he asked.

"He's out on the beach. I think he's doing his devotions."

"M'kay." He slunk down into his seat and sipped his coffee. The pile of food in front of him didn't even entice his appetite.

Ms. Doris laid her small hand on his shoulder and squeezed gently. "What is it, Jack? What's wrong?"

"I found her. I found Candice." Even thinking of her warred with the beast in his heart.

"Who's Candice?" Ms. Doris sat across from him, her hands wrapping around her blue cup of coffee.

"The girl I love." Yes, he still loved her, even though the word ripped into his heart. He'd thought she felt the same, but why then hadn't she said anything when she left?

"Ah, the mysterious girl who sent you here with a broken heart. Tell me about her," Ms. Doris said kindly.

For the next hour, Jack shared their story. The words and emotions poured out of him and left him exhausted by the end of the tale.

"And last night when I confronted her, she couldn't answer me." Those pleading, brown eyes. "I was so hurt. I said words that I can't take back, even though they were the biggest lie I have ever told. I want to be with her. I love her."

"Oh, Jack, sometimes love is like that. It has its ups and downs and hurts and joys. Love can lead us to the highest highs and leave us in the lowest lows. But that's what forgiveness is for. You can't love completely without an equal measure of forgiveness. Isn't that what Jesus asks us to do? Love and forgive?"

Jack nodded, his eyes distant as he thought over her advice.

"And one other thing," she said. "Maybe the next time you speak to her, try to listen to what she has to say before running away. And I mean really listen—listen with your heart, not just your head."

"Thank you, Ms. Doris."

"Go find your girl. I'd bet my hat that you still mean as much to her as she does to you. By the way, are you still planning on running by the hardware store today? I know Bill is hiring now, so perhaps you want to put your name up for consideration."

"Yeah. I don't know how much longer I can keep Christian here before he runs back to Bethel. A job sounds like a good idea. Is it age that made you so wise?"

Ms. Doris laughed. "No, my dear boy, it's God. I've been praying for you since you arrived. I could see the weight that you carried, and I hoped that you would talk to me. Today, God answered my prayer."

"Ms. Doris, you're a gem," Jack smiled warmly and kissed her cheek.

"Oh, you. Eat your breakfast. The hardware store opens at nine."

Christian joined them at the breakfast table, but he seemed preoccupied with something. He kept frowning and then swallowing. He didn't have much to say. Jack let him be. Christian would talk when he was ready.

At nine o'clock sharp, Jack stood outside Westwood Hardware and rapped lightly on the wooden door. There was a clatter of metal on locks, and the door slowly began to rise, bringing into view a tall, broad-shouldered man with blond hair and a wide smile.

"You must be Jack; I just got off the phone with Doris. Come on in. I'm Graham, by the way," the man said.

Stunned, Jack tripped over the low lip of the door and stumbled into a rack of garden rakes. "Yes, that's me." Ms. Doris, the old minx.

"Well, Jack, I need someone in the lumber yard this time of year. It's hard, physical work, but the wage is good. I expect twenty-five hours a week. Can you start tomorrow?"

"Yes, I most certainly can. And thank you," Jack said, unable to believe how blessed he was.

"Great, I'll see you tomorrow at eight-thirty."

Jack shook Graham's hand. Things were working out. The store was close to the beach and Ms. Doris's house, and he'd found the girl his heart wanted. Now, all he had to do was convince Candice to talk to him. A diner across the road caught his eye. A celebratory milkshake sounded like a wonderful way to stave off the balmy heat. He walked over, opened the door, and sat in the nearest booth. He grabbed a menu and studied the contents.

A few minutes later, a familiar voice met his ears. "Hi, my name's Candice. I will be your server today. What can I get you?"

Jack whipped his head up.

No way.

"Candice?"

She looked up from her notepad and backed away from him clumsily. She turned to walk away, and Jack hopped up and walked after her.

"Can we talk, please?" he asked.

Desperately, he reached for her arm. She froze and lifted her head to look at him. Tear-filled eyes met his, a flood of emotions lingering in their depths.

"Haven't you hurt me enough?" she whispered.

His hand fell limply from her arm, and he bowed his head. He deserved that; he totally did. He had to make this right. "Candice, please, *please* can we talk?"

Candice backed further away. "I can't do this with you. You made yourself perfectly clear last night, Jack. I don't think there's anything left to say."

There was plenty still to say, so why couldn't he get the words out? A short lady came to stand in front of him as Candice disappeared out the door.

"I think you need to leave, son," she said, lightly turning him toward the door.

"I need to speak to her. I need to make this right," he pleaded.

"What's your name, son?" the woman asked.

"Jack."

Immediately, her expression shifted. "Well, Jack, it seems we have some talkin' to do." She sent him a motherly smile. "Follow me," she said, indicating an office off to the side of the diner. Jack followed, grasping on to whatever hope he had left. Wherever this lady was leading him, maybe it would bring him some answers regarding Candice and what he could do to show her that he still loved her.

"I'm Daisy, and Candice is a friend of mine. If you want my advice, give her a bouquet of daisies and a proper apology." Daisy walked into the middle of the office, indicating for Jack to take a seat opposite her.

"Come again?"

"Daisies and a proper apology. Candice has told me all about you, Jack. Now, why don't you tell me why the girl who couldn't stop singing your praises to me for the past four months doesn't want to talk to you?"

Jack braced his elbows on his knees and exhaled heavily. "I messed up last night. I don't know what happened. I was so angry and hurt, and I couldn't seem to stop the words before they came out. I love her."

Daisy smiled. "I know you love her, Jack, and I have it on good authority she feels the same. Call her and make this right."

"But I don't have her new number, and I—"

Daisy cut him off, handing him a small piece of paper with a phone number.

"Don't tell her where you got it." She winked at Jack. "Do the right thing, for both of you."

Hope roared like a tidal wave. His heart sped up, his hands suddenly clammy. He breathed in deeply. He could do this.

Jack: *Candice, it's Jack. Please can I talk to you? I'm so sorry. If you could find it in your heart to hear me out, please meet me at Daisy's on Friday night at eight.*

The phone trembled in his hands as he pressed send. With unsteady legs, he walked back out into the diner. Candice hadn't returned yet, and he sighed at the loss. He walked out of the diner and said a prayer. God was only One Who could fix this now.

Candice stumbled down the sidewalk, tears blurring her vision. The anger Jack showed last night was gone, and suddenly, he was desperate to apologize. And she was so confused. Those blue eyes begged for her understanding. But what about what he'd said last night? Had that been a lie?

Suddenly, she remembered the fervent prayer she had said in the dark hours of the night for Jack to return to her life. And now, here he was. The situation wasn't perfect, but now they had the chance to make it work. Jack was here in Westwood, which was something she'd been wishing for and praying about for months.

Her phone pinged in her pocket. It was probably Daisy checking up on her. Settling onto her favorite spot on the beach—the place where she came often to pray and think—she took her phone out. Her heart fluttered when she saw the message on the screen. Thoughts and emotions converged and formed a surge of thankfulness.

I'm trusting You, Lord.

Candice took a deep breath and typed one word: *Okay.*

CHAPTER TWENTY-FOUR

If wooing someone was an Olympic sport, Jack was trying for the gold. Every morning, Candice walked into Daisy's for her shift, and a bouquet of daises would be waiting for her, accompanied by a cute, brown teddy or chocolate or a voucher for hot chocolate at the local coffee shop.

When the lunchtime rush came, Jack walked into the diner, asked to be seated in her section, and ordered a shake or burger or whatever else she suggested that day. Seeing him each day made her look forward to seeing him the next. She'd wait anxiously for one o'clock to arrive and see his tall frame push the door open and smile as soon as he saw her. Sometimes, she could feel his eyes follow her as she moved around the diner. He would only ask how she was and how her day was going. By the time her shift ended on Friday, her anger with Jack had all but disappeared, and she was eager to clear the air and talk to him again.

"You look nice. Where are you off to?" her dad asked when Candice walked down the stairs and into the front room.

Her dad's puzzled expression was one that Candice didn't really know how to handle. Surely, he couldn't know that she was going to meet Jack. Things between them were difficult enough without her father getting involved. She'd tried numerous times to forgive her father, but there was still so much anger and resentment in her about the situation and his part in it. She knew that she needed to pray more about it.

"Just going out," Candice said. She pulled at her long, green A-line dress, smoothing it down so it laid neatly and flattered her baby bump. Jack didn't mind she was pregnant, so she decided to make the best of the situation and knock his socks off. Her long, auburn hair hung down her back, held back by a gold clip given to her by Mrs. Potter for her sixteenth birthday.

Her dad pursed his lips, hesitant. "Okay. You know the drill. Don't be late. No drinking. Be careful and call me if anything happens to you or the baby."

She swallowed the urge to tell him again that she was eighteen and could look after herself. It hadn't helped much last time, so she let it pass.

"Yes, Dad."

The nervous knot in her stomach tightened as she climbed into her car. Her apparent agitation swirled the little body inside her up and down. *Oh, baby.* She rubbed her bump tenderly, hoping to calm her little boy.

Well, it's now or never.

One light remained on in the diner when Candice arrived. Jack's car, Betty, was parked beside Daisy's blue sedan, and a tall, tense figure paced up and down the length of the car. Jack. Her vision misted with tears from the memories that the old, familiar car brought. Jack stopped and turned to her as she brought her car to a stop. He watched her, took two steps, stopped, and then walked toward her again.

"You came," he said, voice thick with relief.

Her pulse sped up. She nodded and climbed out of the car and laid her hand on her stomach, either to stop the butterflies or calm the baby. She wasn't sure which.

"Yes, I came."

Jack's expression changed from relief to sheer awe when he saw her.

"Y-you look absolutely beautiful. Even more beautiful than I remember." He cleared his throat and looked down, and he awkwardly stuffed his hands in his pockets.

"I'm sorry," he said. There was so much hope and sincerity in his words and expression that Candice knew deep down the words he'd said that night on the beach hadn't been true. If anything, Jack had been downright lying. And what of the questions? She'd ask him about them sometime. Her heart tripped over itself.

She smiled, genuine and heartfelt. "I know."

There must have been something in the way she said the words that made the worry in Jack's eyes disappear. He smiled in the way she remembered—the smile that made her pulse race a little faster and gave her the knowledge that she had been right all along.

"Are you ready to go?" he asked. Some of his old confidence returned to his voice. His hands hung easily by his sides, and on occasion, they twitched in her direction.

"We're not going to the diner?"

Jack grinned mischievously. "No, I asked you to meet me here because I wasn't sure what your dad would do if I picked you up at your house." His mood shifted, his voice barely a whisper. "He might steal you away from me again."

The blatant pain in Jack's words broke something inside her. She couldn't help but lay a gentle hand on his arm. "You don't need to worry about him. He doesn't get a say anymore. I'm old enough to make my own decisions." The plea to forgive her father echoed again. "I'm still so angry with him."

His warm hand met hers, and he tangled their fingers together. Their hands fit perfectly, just like they always had. He stared down into her eyes, seeking something.

"I missed you," Jack whispered. His voice was so raw with emotion that she was sure he'd meant to say something else. He led her back to his car and opened the door. "Climb in. I have a surprise for you."

"A surprise other than the fact that you're in Westwood? How did that even happen, by the way?"

"I'll tell you on the road." Jack closed the passenger door, ran to the driver's side, and climbed in.

The same country station played as Jack pulled out of the lot. He hesitantly reached again for her hand, only fully taking it when she didn't pull away. His body visibly relaxed, and he smiled over at her. He looked surprised, like someone who couldn't believe the good fortune with which he'd been blessed.

"So, how is it you came to Westwood?" Candice asked again once they had been driving for some time.

"When you left, things didn't make sense, and life was hard. You were suddenly ripped away from me, and no one had any answers, and I was . . . lost. When graduation was over and the summer began, I was on the internet one evening looking for something to do or a place to go to get away, and my mom suggested Westwood. Something told me to come here. I didn't know why or for what reason, but the feeling wouldn't go away. I knew that this was where I needed to be. So, about a week ago, I convinced Christian to come with me, and here I am. We've been staying with one of my mom's friends, Ms. Doris, ever since."

"It sounds like a fairy tale," Candice said.

"Maybe, but I'm pretty sure it's a God-tale," Jack quipped, although there was so much truth in his statement.

That small, still Voice tingled at the back of her mind. *See, I told you so.*

Jack was right—this was a God-tale. Only God could orchestrate something like this. "Yeah," she said, awestruck. "Yeah, you're right."

"How have you been? How is the baby? I heard someone say at the diner that you're having a boy."

"I'm doing better now. Junior over here keeps growing," Candice said, pointing at her stomach. "I think he's learning gymnastics in the womb the way he jumps and dives all over the place. I finished school a few weeks ago, and, as you know, I am working at Daisy's Diner. Other than that, nothing much has changed. What about you?"

"Definitely much better now." He glanced at her with a smile that melted her heart. "At the moment, I guess I'm seeing where the wind takes me. College is happening in the fall, but I'm not sure if I'm going yet. I took a job at the hardware store, just in case." There was something in that statement that she would remember later when she was alone.

"Where are you taking me?" The curiosity was killing her. Jack had barely been in town a week, and he clearly already knew more about it than she did.

He grinned again. "Don't worry. We're almost there."

The car came to a stop a few minutes later outside an empty cove. The beauty of the view robbed her of her breath as Jack helped her out of the car. Summer in Westwood was beautiful, but there was no comparison to the magnificent view laid out before her. There were bursts of reds, oranges, pinks, and deep purples streaked across the sky in the shadow of the setting sun. Cobalt waves lapped the white shore, and a pair of tall palm trees formed a natural arc in the pale sand. At the center of the arc was a small, wooden table with a white tablecloth. It had been set with places for two people. A red rose rested on one of the white plates. The flicker of candlelight danced over the oval surface and the drink glasses nearby.

"Welcome to Casa del Jack," Jack said with a fond smile. Silently, he took her hand and led her down the beach to the palm trees. He quickly fetched a large, black cooler from the car and set it down next to the table.

"Is it okay if we talk first before we sit down?" he asked.

The waves washed over their feet, burying them in the wet sand. He was agitated by something again. Jack stopped and took a deep breath, and then, he turned toward the shoreline and ran his hand through his hair. When he turned back to face her, waves of emotion rippled across his features. His Adam's apple bobbed up and down.

"I love you." It was a desperate plea that ripped from him. "This was not the way I wanted to tell you, but I've carried this deep inside me for months. And then that night, on the beach"—he exhaled heavily—"I wanted to say something; but I was angry with your father, the situation, and everything that conspired to keep us apart, and my anger came out instead. I'm sorry I hurt you. I didn't mean what I said. I'm not over you. I never was. I fooled myself into believing I was; but all it took was one glimpse of your face, one whisper of your voice, and I knew that I still loved you."

Somehow during Jack's declaration, she'd found herself in his arms. Each word soothed the ache for him inside her.

"Please, forgive me," he whispered and buried his face into her hair, holding her tighter.

"Already done, Jack. I'm sorry, too. I wish I could've explained everything to you before I left. My dad cut me off from everything; he took my phone and my laptop. I tried, Jack. I tried every method I could think of to speak to you, but my dad made sure that didn't happen. You were never a game to me. You were everything to me."

His grip around her tightened as if he were reliving that dark day. "It doesn't matter now. You're here, and I'm here. God brought us back together. That's all that matters."

Her arms found their way around his back, and she pulled herself closer to him. "And I love you, too," she whispered.

Jack held her steady as he slowly lowered his mouth onto hers in a kiss that was both understanding and held a promise. She was home. Jack held her steady, and they stood there on the beach, wrapped in each other's embrace, both thinking the same three words.

Thank You, God.

EPILOGUE

MIT SPRING SEMESTER

"Sorry I'm late. Professor Martin got a bit carried away with coding today," Jack said.

Candice sat, head bowed over her cellphone under the bright afternoon sun. He paused for a moment and watched the way the sunlight rippled over her russet hair. His heart swelled with pride. The last few months had passed with a blurring surrealness that sometimes still left Jack breathless. From Evan's birth to leaving Westwood to starting up at college together, he and Candice had been on quite a journey, and he was looking forward to what was next.

"No problem. Look!" Candice held her phone out to Jack, showing him a picture of a chubby baby with dark brown hair smiling in a blue romper. Baby Evan carried more of Candice's features than his dad's; Jack had always thought so, even on the day Candice had given birth to him.

"How's he doing?" he asked sitting beside her. His arm automatically sild across her shoulders as she leaned into him.

"The Andersons say he's growing well, eating well, but doesn't like to sleep much." She chuckled, but Jack could still see a bit of longing mixed into her joy. Most days, Candice missed Evan, but Jack knew she felt peace about placing him for adoption.

"Are you ready to go? I don't think your dad will be too happy with us if we're late for his birthday barbecue," Jack said. Another blessing had occurred on the day of Evan's birth: Candice's father had finally accepted Jack and given his blessing to their relationship. He'd been their strongest supporter since that day. The relationship with Candice's mother still had its ups and downs, but they took it as it came.

"I doubt he'll say anything. Mrs. Potter would probably say it first." Candice laughed.

Jack slung both their bags over his shoulder, Candice's hand firmly in his. He kissed her head, breathing in her familiar citrus scent as they walked to his truck.

Thank You, Lord.

ACKNOWLEDGMENTS

Firstly, I thank God for giving me this wonderful opportunity to share His love and message. I would also like to thank my husband and my two boys for being understanding when Mommy needs to pull late hours editing and writing. I would like to thank Katie Solomon for her help and guidance during the editing process; thank you for helping me make this the best story it can be. And as always, a big thank you to Ambassador International for taking me on as a debut author and allowing me to take the story God laid on my heart years ago and share it with the world.

NEXT IN THE BETHEL PRIVATE SCHOOL SERIES . . .

Can one decision change your life?

For Amy Carter, a senior at Bethel Private School, life is rarely fair. Her friends are leaving school one by one, her parents are on the precipice of divorce, and she is currently failing more classes than she'd like. But that isn't the worst of it. She has a secret. A darkness in her mind that haunts her night hours and is only kept at bay by partying, hooking up and lying through her teeth.

When the challenges she faces gradually begin caving in on each other Amy becomes overwhelmed and takes the only way out she can see. Her life at the edge of a shard of glass.

Brad Thorn is messed up, even he will admit it. One step away from jail and carrying the weight of his father's expectations on his shoulders, he hides his regrets by drinking them away.

When the two meet at Heavenly Haven they have no hope for change. But God has other ideas.

Gradually through the love and acceptance of Counselors Griffin and Mildred they learn to accept the mistakes of their past and find forgiveness in the arms of a Savior who expects nothing more from them than their love.

You Found Me
BETHEL PRIVATE SCHOOL SERIES | BOOK THREE

For more information about
Michelle Dykman
and
Someone Like You
please visit:

www.michelledykman.com

For more information about
AMBASSADOR INTERNATIONAL
please visit:

www.ambassador-international.com

Thank you for reading this book. Please consider leaving us a review on your favorite retailer's website, Goodreads or Bookbub, or our website.

In *Addy of the Door Islands*, Judy DuCharme continues the saga of the fascinating people of the Door Islands at the tip of Door County, Wisconsin. Set in the late-1800s, Addy of the Door Islands shares the story of two amazing orphan girls who just want to be loved. Through their story, learn more about the islands and the children who were part of the history of the Orphan Train.

Lyndie is starting her senior year at the College of Charleston, living the life every girl wants in their college years. She is a beautiful, independent woman who is coming to terms with starting life in the real world. She meets Brantley, a guy who talks about God as if they are best friends. After a trip home, can Lyndie to deal with the secret that she thought she had left behind her?

When Rune's worldview is shattered after a false god fails to deliver on a promise, she begins to seek out the legend of Avian: the One, true God. In a parallel journey, a young man in another kingdom, Rolf, wars against the voices of good and evil in his life, all while seeking the one Truth. Their paths soon collide, and together the pair struggle against the alliance of evil that seeks to end their journey to Avian.

www.ingramcontent.com/pod-product-compliance
Lightning Source LLC
Chambersburg PA
CBHW070516260626
47161CB00004B/1568